My Summer of Discontent

My Summer of Discontent

Kenneth Walker

Library of Congress Control Number:		2018913671
ISBN:	Hardcover	978-1-9845-6652-2
	Softcover	978-1-9845-6651-5
	eBook	978-1-9845-6650-8

Print information available on the last page.

Rev. date: 11/16/2018

To order additional copies of this book, contact:
Xlibris
1-888-795-4274
www.Xlibris.com
Orders@Xlibris.com
787484

Dedicated to my wonderful family, friends, and the game of basketball that made My Summer of Discontent possible.

Special thanks to the Veggie Writers and Red Bird/Red Oak writing groups for helping me find my voice through the written word.

Heartfelt Special Thanks to the following people:

My Mama Ernestine Walker RIP

Leslie David Polk RIP

John Schissler

Barbara Branch

PROLOGUE

The minnows in the shallow water of the Milwaukee River drifted over our bare feet. I felt as small as those little creatures that were all colors of the rainbow. My best friend, Smokey Bivens mostly talked about "jumping" into the wide and wild river. He liked to take risks. I didn't.

We usually rolled up the cuffs on our pants to dip our feet into the water. They cooled ankle deep between the rocks on the shore after long bike rides to Estabrook Park. But Smokey liked to venture farther off shore near the rapids. He had rested his dirty once white Converse tennis shoes and threadbare socks neatly on the boulder that overlooked the water. It was not a slippery rock, and he had no trouble climbing it or coming down its rough surface. The only way he could hurt himself was if he leapt off it towards the river. I usually set my socks and shoes next to our bikes on the grass.

It was a tranquil place way before I knew what tranquil meant. All I know was that I felt like a freed black boy when I was in that park. It was like being on level ground, rather than an uneven one in the neighborhood where life was sometimes shaky. We had come to this place since we were little boys when we got our first bicycles.

The lush green trees tried to hide cardinals, blue jays, and sparrows that teased me from seeing their vibrant colors. As they flew into the air I wished that I could have taken flight too. Colorful bugs and butterflies, especially the monarchs, fluttered in the air dodging beaks of hungry birds. The air was fresh and sweet, spring day scents different from our neighborhood.

I studied the beauty and the peacefulness of the place, so I could daydream about being here when things got chaotic in my life. I could enjoy nature and forget where I grew-up, if only for a short time. Smokey loved the park too, but he would never say so. Usually black boys didn't share their feelings much with each other, especially if the topics were birds, flowers, and love.

I don't think Smokey could appreciate the beauty outside himself. And talking about the comfort of nature was one of those things. The park was a place where we could empty our thoughts about the turmoil of growing up in poverty. I guess the park was our stress reliever when we were boys, though we didn't know it at the time. I don't think Smokey knew how to appreciate that feeling. We didn't have to have any money to enjoy the peace of the place, and there was nothing to buy here anyway.

Smokey was rather somber on the last day we came to the park together a couple of weeks before junior high graduation. I knew why he was a little sad, but we didn't talk about it. Normally he was energetic and ready to explore other places in Estabrook Park. We would talk about basketball or the excitement of our upcoming commencement. Smokey loved that damn sharkskin colored suit for the special occasion that I told him not to buy. We had saved enough money from snow shoveling the past winter to get new bikes. And even though his bike was almost broke down, he spent his money on a suit. Anyway he knew he looked good in that suit. I agreed.

I asked him, "Why'd his black ass spent money on church clothes when he never went to church, so where else you going to wear that suit?"

"Mercer, I can do anything I want with my goddamn money," was his answer.

While Smokey took in the scenery of the deep foliage on the opposite shoreline, it was like he was thinking of something else to say to me. He couldn't apologize to me for his angry outburst; it was an unwritten code for black boys not to say I'm sorry.

"Mercer, I don't believe in God."

I thought, where in the hell did this come from? How did he just go from a suit and bike to talking about God? But I just listened to him.

"Man, nobody has ever seen God. He's in someone else's imagination. He never showed himself to me, and you either. Look Mercer, you go to church must Sundays, and I never go, but we still in the same shit together. We both poor and stay hungry most of the time. Black people don't have a damn thing worth anything. This park is close to heaven as we ever gonna get. And we only get a taste of this place only once and awhile. And that is if the white boys don't chase us out. It seems like white folks got it made, just look at the damn houses they live in, and this park are their backyards. We go outside our houses and see and smell garbage. Mercer, we livin' in hell, and that is bullshit.

"You right Smokey," nodding in agreement to his words.

"And you know the butcher, that white bastard Hog Hoffmann owns our house. When Mama can't pay the rent, he comes by looking to get screwed. Man, I am so tired of being called 'nigger' by white and black folks. And you know some of our teachers think Negro kids are stupid as them rocks you constantly looking at."

I laughed out loud, so did Smokey.

"Smokey it ain't going to always be like this. Man, I know it is going to get better for us, but that don't happen overnight."

"Yeah, you're right, and I look so good in that sharp- ass suit. At least when I go to graduation, I'll look good and feel good for once walking across that stage. What you going to do ride your new bike across it?"

We laughed again, and that seemed to lift Smokey's spirit. And I understood why he bought the suit. The topic of suit versus bike never came up again.

Chapter 1

The smells coming through the porch screen made me less angry than I wanted to be. My mother was making fried green tomatoes, scrambled eggs with commodity cheese from the welfare food depot, and slab bacon. My belly growled. And she promised me I could have a cup of coffee, even though she often told me "that coffee makes you blacker." I had earned my breakfast with that morning. Mama made me wheel my rusty red wagon all over the goddamn neighborhood.

I was the only slave in Milwaukee. I dragged brown cartons and silver cans of food from the welfare depot and vegetables from the farmers market. It seemed like I rolled over every crack on the sidewalk, and every bump in the street. I was used to it.

A girl I liked a lot joined us with bundles of neck bones wrapped in butcher paper from Hog Hoffmann's meat shop. She liked to flirt with me, but when she plopped the bundles on the wagon without permission, I wanted to say, "what the hell, you can carry your damn neck bones." My mother looked at me like I was going to say aloud what I was thinking. Mama dared me with her eyes to say something.

I knew that look well and kept my thoughts to myself, even after dropping off my friend near her house on the way to mine.

After we unloaded the food from my Red Flyer wagon at our kitchen table, I returned it to the basement. I headed out from the back door to the front porch. My mother and friend had irritated me enough on that Saturday morning. I just wanted to sit alone on my porch.

It was the warmest day of spring, and Smokey borrowed my bike to ride with Gaddis and Licorice, friends that my father said were "always up to no good." But I couldn't go to the park that morning.

The warm breeze felt so good, as it flowed over my sweaty body. The spring air smelled sweet and sunshine made me feel free again, especially after being held prisoner inside my cigarette smelling house most of winter. Quarrelling blue jays and the noisy kids at play on the dirt lawn in front of Smokey's house were signs that summer was near. The fragrances of the purple lilac bushes helping me relax. There were budding green leaves on trees and yellow dandelions on lawns which brought back color to the block after being covered with grey snow and ice. I started to feel better.

Two black and whites rolled up in front of Smokey's house. It always was bad news when cops came to the block. There were at least three bikes sticking out the trunks of both cars; two in the rear cop car and one in the front.

Gaddis Hopgood and Licorice Brown sat stiff in the rear cop car seat as if they were in handcuffs. I looked for Smokey in the other car but didn't see his head of curly black hair. I bet Smokey broke his ass falling off my bike.

Gaddis and Licorice exited the rear doors of the car. Their faces were dripping wet, like it did after we played basketball on the playground. But it wasn't that hot of a day to sweat like that to me.

Both boys grabbed their bikes out of the trunk of the vehicle they were sitting in, and walked unsteadily as they wheeled their bikes to the sidewalk in front of Gaddis's house. I got this sick feeling inside watching them. This was more serious than Smokey falling off my bike.

I turned my attention away from my friends to watch a tall cop dressed in full blues talking to Smokey's mother through her screen door. I wondered what was going on. I knew Smokey's mother would pitch-a-fit if Smokey had gotten into trouble.

A hefty cop with a round pink face took my bike out of the trunk of the front cop car. He asked my friends something I couldn't hear, but they pointed their fingers at me like I'd done something wrong. Then I got scared. *What could I have done wrong besides loaning Smokey my bike?*

The big stomached cop with the police hat that didn't fit right took his time wheeling my bike to the front steps of my house. My Mama had come to the porch screen door to tell me to come and eat. She saw the cop with my bike on the sidewalk. A confused look came over her face. She stepped onto the porch. Mama didn't like the police. The cop's eyes were red. He looked like people I'd seen stumble out the corner taverns sometimes. He was sweating badly and he reeked of beer that I could smell from where I stood.

"Those boys, those boys over there, said this bike is yours." His words mumbled out of his mouth.

Before I could answer him, a scream so powerful rang out that the birds stopped twittering, children froze at play, and scents in the air ceased to exist. People came out of their houses to see what was going on. It was as if the world had stopped moving. It was a perfectly, horrible scream, and it frightened me.

Smokey's mother rushed out the door and brushed past the uniformed cop, almost knocking him over as she leapt over the porch steps without touching them. She was wild and in a frenzy, and looked around to run somewhere, but there was nowhere to run to. Her children on the dirt lawn grabbed at her clothes and started tugging at what they could hold on to. Smokey's mother started screaming, "My baby is gone" and "Lord have mercy!" "Why'd you take my baby away from us?" Realizing what was wrong, the seven kids around her started crying with their mother and screamed with a grief that filled the air. I'd never felt words before that powerful. Smokey's mother grabbed her children as best she could, but they seemed to be holding her upright as they walked up the rickety steps of their porch. Now they entered the house as one person, miffed in grief.

"What happened?" My mother asked the dispassionate cop with my bike.

The cop put the kick-stand down on the bike on the sidewalk before he spoke. He looked at us and said, "There was an accident at Estabrook Park this morning. A boy drowned. According to those two boys across the street, he came to the park on this bike. The police pulled his body out of the water about a mile downstream."

There was no hint of caring in his voice which deep inside I wouldn't hear from a white man. I was stunned, like I'd been hit in the chest with a sledge hammer. It hurt so badly. The fat cop didn't even mention Smokey's name. He just turned around and stumbled back to his car. What I heard coming out of the sloppy cop's mouth in my mind was that Smokey was just another nigger that had lost his life and so what?

I hated him. And I thought I couldn't hate anyone.

I cried uncontrollably like a newborn baby coming out of the womb and being slapped hard on the ass by a doctor. Smokey's dead! It was the cruelest joke I'd ever heard. But death could never be a lie. I began to choke. It was difficult to take in air. I couldn't breathe. My mother had tears running down her chestnut colored cheeks. I'd never seen her cry before. She wrapped her big arms around my head and squeezed it tightly against her chest. She stroked my head with her rough hands that now felt so gentle. She whispered to me that, "everything's going to be alright." I wasn't sure. Because I knew my broken heart would never heal.

Gaddis and Licorice came across the street once the cops had left the block. I guess they wanted to explain to me what happened that morning at the park. I wasn't in the mood to hear what they had to say and I didn't care what happened at the park. Whatever they were going to tell me wasn't going to bring back my best friend. They should have saved him. I lost three friends on that day.

I pulled away from my mother's strong arms. I didn't want her to ever hold me against her bosom like that again. I turned my back on my former friends and headed indoors to eat. My appetite was gone and I headed to my bedroom to cry.

My mother had stayed on the porch to listen to what the boys had to say. She later told me that Gaddis did all the talking about what happened. It was like Licorice was too scared to speak. I never told my mother, but Gaddis, the church boy, was the biggest liar I'd ever known.

Smokey had now escaped Milwaukee a city we both detested since we were little boys. We had always wanted to run off to California where there was sunshine and warmth every day. I don't think Smokey imagined he'd die before he got there. I never imagined it either.

Chapter 2

I had known Gaddis Hopgood since I was four years old. And over the years growing up I had sat my feet under their dinner table a numerous of times. By the time I was eleven years old the brood of siblings had reached nine with Gaddis being the middle child. Gaddis's parents treated me like I was one of their children. Every time I ate food at their house there always seemed to have a feast. There were many times when there were platters of chicken and ribs; bowls of potato salad and green beans with ham hocks; pans of macaroni and cheese and pitchers of sweet tea or Kool Aid to wash everything down. The deserts, fried apple or peach pies and German chocolate cake. I was in *food heaven.* The Hopgood's one meal could feed our family for a week. Almost every one of Gaddis's siblings was heavyset and was happy-go-lucky. I loved them all like they were my family.

When Smokey's family moved to the block when I was about seven years old, Smokey and I we became fast friends, Gaddis seemed jealous of that friendship. Smokey and I had more in common. We had the freedom to roam and play in the streets or alleys with other kids whenever we wanted. Smokey and I loved sports, especially basketball. Gaddis's life was tied to the Pentecostal church on the corner where his father was a deacon. Four or five times a week, Gaddis was in church while me and Smokey were playing or riding our bikes everywhere we could in the city with other kids. What I think irritated Gaddis most was that me and Smokey could go to the movies and dances with girls and participate in supervised sports in school. His religion didn't allow Gaddis to do those things. I don't think Gaddis forgave me and Smokey for leaving him behind.

Chapter 3

I hated our cramped bathroom. It was a frightening place. I could take two short steps and be at the bath tub. The tiniest sink was sandwiched between the tub and the toilet. I didn't turn on the overhead light because I didn't want to see the cockroaches or cracks in the faded blue paint of the walls. Something scurried across my bare feet as I flushed the toilet, but I had gotten used to creepy crawly things in my house, I then felt for the gummy soap on the sink top and turned on the hot water faucet, but out came cold water.

The slight smell of urine hovered in the air, even though my mother had recently cleaned it. I felt for the damp towel that hung over the side of the tub, and dried my hands as best as I could. There was light coming through the cracks of the floor from the basement. Someone had forgotten to turn off the light.

I walked out into the hall next to the kitchen and saw my father sitting under the dim light at the kitchen table. He was next to an open window.

He had to have seen me? But he didn't utter a word.

The kitchen smelled of gun oil and stale beer. A Camel cigarette dangled from his mouth and the smoke from it hovered over his head like a cloud. There was static of his transistor radio sitting on the window sill. It was broadcasting the Braves and Dodger baseball game from County Stadium. A can of *Blatz* beer stood next to a jelly jar cap of cigarette butts.

The cigarette smoke made my eyes water. And the strong odors from the oil and beer made my stomach grumble. But I wasn't going back into that bathroom until the morning if I could help it.

He did not acknowledge me standing there looking at him. But my father seldom noticed me, unless he wanted to order me to do something.

Friday night was my father's gambling night. There was always money to gamble with, but never any money to fix anything in our dreary house. The refrigerator and pantry shelves were never full of stuff to eat. He didn't seem to notice or care.

I was tired of having holes in my underwear and in the soles of my tennis shoes. Yet, Daddy had a closet full of colorful suits and sports coats, with shiny shoes lined-up beneath them on the floor.

I knew that my mother, my sister Birdie, and I probably would not see him until Sunday evening. I loved my father, but I wondered why I was supposed to care about him.

My father's hair was a wavy ink black that pressed down on his head. And his skin was smooth tan-brown. He had brown eyes like mine. Other than that we looked nothing alike. He was handsome;

probably better looking than I'd ever be. I was only ten years old, and my intuition told me that good looking people didn't worry about anyone but themselves. All I wanted was to grow up to be a better man than the man at the kitchen table.

A brown Stacey Adams shoe box lay before him on the table on newspaper. He kept his guns in that box. Bullets were set up like tiny missiles at the edge of the paper. A derringer and a twenty-two caliber revolver lay on a greasy brown paper bag. A canister of Burkes Gun Oil, a couple of bronze bore brushes, and a clean red rag covered the rest of the newspaper. He gave those guns more attention than he ever gave me.

Daddy took the cigarette out of his mouth, gently laid it at the side of jelly jar cap and slugged down his beer. He picked up the revolver and stroked the bore brush in and out of the barrel of the gun. Once he was done with the brush, he put oil on the red rag and gently caressed it over the chrome part of the revolver.

Even though they didn't itch I scratched my arms and legs while looking at him. He still ignored me. I headed back to my bedroom out of his sight. My father started talking by the time I reached the open door of my room. I wanted to disregard his words, but I knew better.

"I heard you an' Smokey got into a fight with some boys down the block today," he said while rubbing on his guns still not facing me. "Your mama said you both got your asses kicked." My father didn't press me for an explanation of the fight. He just kept cleaning his guns.

Why does Mama have to tell Daddy every goddamn thing I get into during the day? What in the hell was I supposed to say him?

I didn't want to talk to my father. He never wanted to hear anything I had to say anyway. He did like to give me lectures though, which were worse than any whooping from my mother. My conversations with my father were always one-sided. I could never express what was on my mind.

My father was right; we did get slapped around a bit. I didn't tell him that it was four older boys against Smokey and me. We didn't run away from the fight. I probably would have run home if Smokey hadn't of been with me. He wasn't afraid of anyone. Smokey had my back, and I had his. We wouldn't let each other be afraid of anybody while we were together.

I stood in the hall and stared at him. Daddy never looked up from his guns. I know he didn't care whether I got my ass kicked or not. Maybe I just wasn't important enough for him to say anything to me.

My father let the cigarette dangle from his mouth as he said, "You never know when some niggah want to start some shit with me when I'm out. I take a gun or two just so he knows where I stand."

It seemed like he was talking to himself.

He looked at me for the first time since I stepped out of the bathroom.

Daddy said to me in a tone that gave me a chill, "let me tell you somethin' Mercer Bevenue." My father always called me by my full name whenever he wanted my full attention. "If I ever catch you messing with guns, I will beat you to within an inch of your life."

The thought of having a gun never crossed my mind until that night. But my father's words stuck with me. It wasn't his threat of the razor strap beating. I just couldn't see myself being like my father, settling fights with guns.

As disinterested as my father seemed be about my existence, I felt safe under his roof. Although our house was in shambles most of time because Daddy didn't commit enough money to the household. He made sure that my mother carried out his orders about disciplining me and my sister Birdie to keep us in line. Birdie, her given name was Anna Blanch, which she hated. So I gave her the nickname Birdie because she liked to watch *Tweetey Bird* in cartoons on Saturday mornings. My sister and I weren't allowed to curse or talk back or interrupt while adults were talking. My slapped me one time because I said "darn," she said it sounded too much like "damn." Mama used profanity all the time. But in our house it was *do as I say not as I do.*

There was a curfew for me until I was about thirteen years old. I can still hear Daddy talking to me, always the same words; "Mercer, when it gets dark outside, you better have your ass on the front porch before them street lights came on." It I broke curfew Mama would give me a whooping.

My father wanted to know who my friends were and where I went with them. If Daddy didn't approve of certain friends, he would say so. If we Negro kids went to white people's neighborhoods, he knew it could mean trouble for us. He didn't trust white people to do "right by colored kids." I thought that I had the right to go anywhere I wanted to go. My father disapproved of my attitude about freedom of movement in this city for "colored folks.".

Chapter 4

Winter is a cold bitch and *summer was a hot one,* according to Smokey. It was like he was cursing a person and not a season. He wanted every day to be perfect. I hated winter just as much as he did. When the summer heat came around I never complained. Somehow in warm weather I felt so worthy of being alive. During winter months I felt like I was hibernating like a bear in my house. Cold weather usually froze everything outside, and in a sense everything inside my mind. It was an enemy I could not defeat. Yet, when there was snow on the ground, Smokey and I could make some money shoveling it for people.

There were few birds that braved the cold, except for pigeons that pecked around trash on snow covered lawns. Nor were there sweet fragrances to smell from colorful flowers or green leaves that waved at me from trees when warm breezes blew through them. I missed summer every winter.

Outdoors, the landscape looked like a black and white movie. There were lifeless naked trees with branches that seem to be reaching for something in the gray sky. The houses in the neighborhood were drab and almost colorless. I spent so much time worrying about keeping warm in winter that I found it hard to thrive in its presence.

I hated to venture outside in the harsh elements of winter. A poor black kid like me had no choice. I had to go to school and run errands for my mother with little protection from the cold. In the heat of summer the only clothing I usually needed was a tee-shirt and a pair of shorts. The winter clothing I wore was a burden physically and mentally; I had to have boots, thick sweat socks, gloves, and a hooded coat, and if I was lucky, a wool hat to cover my ears. And maybe even Long Johns, if Mama could afford to get me a pair. I sometimes had to wear two pair of pants just to keep my legs warm. It was a chore to get ready to face the force of winter, especially if I knew that my clothing wasn't going to keep me warm. It often brought tears to eyes when I had to go outside. The only thing that warmed me up a little was shoveling snow, and only then if I was going to make some change doing it. It kept my mind off how cold I was.

Smokey thought that if we moved to California it would be our salvation from the life we had here, and all our problems of being black and poor would disappear in the sunshine. California was probably the only state he could identify on a map. This *escape* from cold weather was not Smokey's only reason for wanting to leave, but it was the one he talked about the most. Smokey wanted a fresh start to life. I did too. And I wondered *how many black boys in other cities like ours also looking for a fresh towards a better start in California?*

———————

The sky was overcast at noon. And we walked like bent silhouettes westward against the gale of the blowing snow. A strong wind pummeled us with sleet that formed icy crusts on our winter clothing. The crunchy sounds of boots striking the dense snow on the ground, and the shrill of the arctic-like wind dominated the sounds in the air. The blinding snow blurred visions as we tried to walk in each other's footsteps. Our winter routine for our group of friends was to walk to and from school together like this since kindergarten in all kinds of weather.

I was glad it was Friday. It was a ten block walk from Robert Fulton junior high to our neighborhood. Phoebe, Smokey, Gaddis, and me lived on the same block. But Gaddis often took the city bus when the weather was bad. He was the only thirteen year-old that seemed to always have money. Gaddis was selfish he never shared anything with us, especially money. Pumpkin and Licorice lived about two blocks past our street.

I hoped spring was just around the corner. It was late March, and I felt like a walking *Fudgesicle* chocolate ice cream bar in winter clothing. We were in an icy storm, but tomorrow could be the start of a heat wave. The weather was unpredictable just like life to me. Junior high and the routine of walking to school in winter would be over in a couple of months. The moments with friends walking home together would be coming to an end. A little sad for me, but Smokey was ecstatic to move beyond our group of friends. He always felt that nostalgia was for *suckers.* I guess I was one of them.

I never admitted that I liked having friends. In my mind growing up, I needed to have fun in my life. With friends around I never felt lonely. And expect they felt the same although no one would say so. There was a lot of our turmoil in our lives that stemmed from being impoverished. Yet, when we were interacting with each other the sadness we felt as poor kids feel strong and our spirits were always lifted when were together outside our homes.

I hoped to get home to a heated house. I did remember that Mama said that if the weather held up, she was going to go to the grocery store near our house. So, if she wasn't there, then I could predict that I was going into a frigid house. A mound of heavy snow covered the bottom half of the side door to my house. I kicked heavy snow away with my rubber boots, and pushed to open the unlocked door. The stairs moaned when my boots landed on the old wood. I took my gloves off. My fingers looked like short boiled brown hot dogs. The frost covered parka I wore was heavy as I placed it on a hook on the wall. I pushed the flimsy kitchen door open. No one was home and the house was freezing. *I guess Mama did go to the store.*

Many people did not lock their doors in my Milwaukee neighborhood, usually no matter the season. It was too cold and snowy most days in winter for breaking into houses. And taking out a key to get in cold weather was inconvenient; besides there were no clear getaways for thieves with snow and ice on the ground. Most of all, there was nothing of value worth taking in my house, with the exception of my bike.

I flipped on the light switch of the kitchen to startle the cockroaches. But there were no roaches anywhere when the light came on. It was the first time that I could remember that those nasty insects weren't there when I lights flickered on. I could only imagine where they were hiding. I turned on our olive green gas stove, and lit the pilot light with a wooden match from a box on the kitchen table, bending down on elbows and knees to put the match flame to the pilot light. It lit on the first try this time. I turned on the oven and eyes of the stove for heat. And the smell of gas from it made me a little queasy.

The floor was a little grimy from the snow and dirty ice I tracked in with my boots. I dragged a dinette chair and sat in it in front of the opened oven door to warm up a little. My feet were numb, even in my thick socks inside my shoes. I dried my boots with a kitchen towel which I knew my mother would get angry about it. I wiped up the floor as best that I could and threw the towel in the back hall. I figured my mother wouldn't be so upset with me if the kitchen was warm, heat made everything better.

There was a loosely covered Maxwell House coffee can on the stovetop. As the bacon and grease drippings in it warmed, my mouth began to water. At that point, I wondered where my mother was. I hoped she had gone to the grocery store. I found it hard to worry about Mama because she was the toughest woman I knew, even most men that I came across in my world. Yet, I worried that the weather was a thing that she couldn't defeat. Mama usually went grocery shopping on Saturday if there was enough money to buy food. Wherever she was, I'd better have the house warm when she got here especially since I was home before her.

There wasn't much food in the house except for a few boxes of beans, oatmeal, and a tin of spam of the pantry shelves from the welfare food depot, mostly food that I didn't know how to cook. I was disappointed in the choices I had to eat. And my mother would be upset if I opened any food without her supervision. My father went down South with his brothers to Covington, Tennessee, his hometown, but he took Birdie. I wanted to go too. But my father had told me emphatically "no" when I asked him if I could go too.

"Mercer, you can get away with talkin' to white folks like you do up here, but down there those white people will lynch your black ass just for lookin' at them funny. I see how you act around white and coloreds' up here, like you better than they are, talking slick to them. Well, in the South that shit don't wash. Anyway you got to take care of your mama." he told me. *Don't you mean that Mama needed to take care of me,* is what I wanted to say to Daddy? I knew better than try and correct his words. I never thought that my father felt had faith in me to take care of myself, yet alone my mother.

It was like he didn't want to tell me that I couldn't go South with them. In hindsight it was probably Daddy's way of trying to protect me. I had no idea there was a way to look at *white folks* down South that was any different than where we lived. It was also disheartening to know that my father couldn't keep me safe where he grew up.

I knew about racism living in Milwaukee, it had shown its ugly face almost everywhere I went in this city. My father was right about me that I would never accept that anyone was better than me because of the color of their skin. The places that white people lived in the city could be anywhere they wanted to live. The majority of black people lived in the inner city, no matter of their economic status. I went to neighborhood public schools which people segregated for the most part with a sprinkling of white kids in the classrooms. And most of the businesses and houses were owned by white people in the community. It wasn't that I didn't like going to those schools or being a customer at some those stores, it was so just that there was an uneven divide to what existed between the races in the city in which I lived; My school didn't have a gymnasium big enough to have home games in basketball. The white schools had large gyms with bleachers with regulation bright and shiny courts. Our teams rarely lost games when we played there. And I always imagined whether we could have won every basketball game if we had the resources like those white schools.

There were few jobs where we lived. My father had to get up early in the morning to go to his factory job on the south side of the city. Many times he would walk miles to get to work if he didn't have bus fare or couldn't get a ride. He seldom missed work. My father always said that "colored folks are the last hired and the first fired, no matter how hard we work." He had to back out of the south side because of the unwritten or written, *sundown law,* just like down South. The *law* allowed cops or residence to harass anyone with *wrong* skin color. I felt no need to go where I wasn't wanted. And I certainly wasn't going to be a factory worker when I grew up, at least I thought that way when I was young.

———————

The tattered couch and makeshift curtains in his living room insufficiently blocked the wintry wind coming through the sills and the crack in the picture window of the living room. Hopefully, the snow would let up so Smokey and I could go snow shoveling to make some money.

I looked between the dingy blue bed sheets that hung over a clothesline rope to see if Smokey was outside his house shoveling, but the big cracked picture window was too frosted over to see through it. The c*urtains* were attached by nails on the frames on either side of the window. The cold air whistled through the opening of the curtain with gusto. The snow was still falling like icy bullets outside. I could hear mother's voice in my mind, *Mercer, close those goddamn curtains, you lettin' in cold.* I closed the curtains and went back to the kitchen to turn off the stove and closed the oven door. I needed to do that because the stove wasn't to be used to heat a house. Plus my mother was afraid that a fire could start in the house or that gas would seep into the air. And I knew that the first thing she would do when she got home was to light a cigarette.

In the basement there was coal in the bin for a change. I took the matches and some old newspapers from stack in the hall and headed to the furnace. It took ten minutes to shovel coal and light it with the newspaper. Like the cockroaches in the kitchen, the rats and mice stayed out of sight by the furnace. The drafty house would take a long time to heat up.

My parka coat and gloves were still frosty, almost stiff, but I had to shovel snow in front and the side of the house before my mother came home. I grabbed the snow shovel from the dirty wall and headed out into winter looking for Smokey to go shovel snow for other people on Third Street.

There were a lot of businesses on Third owned by Italians, Jews, and Germans. It was a street where most of the black people shopped. The Germans always paid well, while the Italians and Jewish businesses where looking for *slave* labor. So, Smokey and I had to negotiate the terms before we did any work. For example; a business owner would say, "I'll give you five dollars to shovel the sidewalk and the parking lot in the back." We had to make sure that it was five dollars apiece not together. Or else we'd shovel a lot of snow for nothing. If we didn't get paid fairly, Smokey and I would come back and shovel snow back onto the sidewalk or the parking lots. It was easy dumping the snow back than shoveling it up. But we never had to do that with the Germans, they owned the few bakeries on the street. If we did a good job they would give us free pastries, even enough to take home after we were paid.

———————

Smokey came outside while I was finishing up around my house. *I bet he waited until I was almost done with my shoveling so I'd help him with his.* I should have gone back in the house while he shoveled around his house, but I didn't. I let him know that I knew what he did. All he would say was "I don't know what you talkin' about Mercer," with a sly smile on his face.

It had gotten late and the snow was still falling.

"Man, I got some shit do for my mother before I can make some bucks," said Smokey not too happily. I know it hurt for him to say that, for he loved money more than I did.

"Yeah Smokey, I can't go until my Mama comes back to the house. Plus it's getting late and the snow is still coming down. The stores on Third are probably going to close early in this weather. And we probably going to have to come back out and shovel again. This time I'm going to wait until you finish before I come outside so your black-ass can help me." We laughed loudly as we stood next to each other shovels in hand.

"We can go early in the morning before the stores open. You know them white folks got to have those sidewalks clear so those black folks can get in the door to spend their money," said Smokey.

"That's fine with me, man. I need to warm up in my house, but I doubt that is possible. I'll check you out later. I am hungry, thirsty, and tired as hell. And I am hoping Mama gets home before it gets dark." I headed back across the street to my house, but I had to keep an eye out for Smokey. The snow was wet enough to make good snowballs and he was known to throw them at me. Sure enough, Smokey had dropped his shovel, and was stooping down to make a snowball. I picked up a shovel full of snow and ran as close to him and heaved the heavy white stuff on his head. By the time he brushed off I was laughing at my side door to my house. It was a thing I did to get him before he got me. I'm sure Smokey thought the same. I always felt that I was learning a lesson that I should never turn my back on friend or foe.

I was hoping to quench my thirst but the water that came out of the faucet dripped slowly. It took awhile for the glass to fill up. And it looked like weak coffee. But I had nothing else to drink. The water faucets in my house had to be left on when it below freezing days so the water pipes wouldn't freeze-up. There were little icicles that hung from the water pipes in the basement. Once the house warmed up the water would flow better.

I sat on my raggedy coach in front of the black and white TV watching *Father Knows Best.* The mother in the show cooked dinner for her family in a colorful apron in my imagination. The father comes home and the wife kisses him and takes his overcoat and gather around him. And the children greet him like they were happy to see him. The house looked warm and cozy. It was a scene that didn't reflect anything I'd ever experienced in a black home, especially mine. I sat there in a heavy warm sweater, thick sweat socks, and a pair of corduroy pants over my Long Johns. I wondered if I was going to shed these clothes when I went to bed.

Chapter 5

"Damn man, all your relatives are ugly," Smokey said after looking at my family's frayed photo album.

"I'm going to tell my mama you said that. She won't be feeding your black ass anymore fried chicken and potato salad on Sundays anymore," I said.

"Aw Mercer, you know I was just foolin' around."

"Yeah, I bet. Besides I ain't seen anyone cute up in your house."

We both chuckled. I think we were about twelve years old as we sat in my living room waiting for my mother to come back home so I could go outside. To keep from being bored, we looked at photos, mostly black-and-white ones in the thick album. There were also some framed ones scattered around the house that Smokey wanted to see up close.

Smokey was fascinated with the photos of strangers. There weren't any photos hanging on walls or on coffee tables in his house that I ever saw. I remember feeling sad about that, thinking that my friend probably had no idea of what his extended family looked liked.

"My father is dead," is what Smokey said whenever the topic came up in a conversation with friends. He didn't want them to call him a *bastard*. He was *legitimate* to me before I knew what the word meant. And Smokey knew he'd be treated better if he weren't a bastard. We never talked much about it. He must have decided his father was "dead" because he wasn't a part of his life, though he knew his father was somewhere alive in Louisiana.

Smokey had light caramel-colored skin and a head full of black curly hair. He didn't look like any of his six step brothers and sisters, or his sister from the same father. All the other children had the same mother but different fathers. None of the siblings had their mother's physical features or the same skin color. Smokey didn't favor any of his siblings. They all had different fathers, but his sibs looked the same. His *real* sister was a year younger. If all the siblings walked down the street together, anyone looking at them would not guess that they were related.

Smokey's sister had ebony colored skin. She had long shoulder length black hair. She was beautiful to me. There was no girl in our neighborhood that looked like her. Lighter-skinned people were thought of as more attractive in the streets and alleys where we played.

When I was young, I didn't discriminate against any girl that would talk to me. It didn't matter if the girl was light or dark-skinned, or all skin colors in-between. They all were good looking in my eyes. I wasn't lucky like Smokey. All the girls were all over him because he was handsome. I was just glad girls would have mercy on me by giving me some attention when he was around.

I went to my parents' bedroom to get my favorite photo. It was an eight-by-ten sepia toned photo, taken in the late 1930's, according to my mother. The photo captured Smokey's full attention. It was in a sturdy dark-wood frame that was always on top on my mother's Chester of drawers, as she called the good looking piece of furniture. I was proud to show it to Smokey. The two people in the frame were my mother's parents. I told him that my grandfather passed away couple of years before I was born.

"Hey Mercer, your grandpa looks just like you, except without the nappy hair you got on your big head."

"I may have a big head, but your ears are like *Dumbo the Flying Elephant*. In fact you probably need to fly your black ass back across the street."

"Okay, okay, okay, man, you know I was only ribbing you," Smokey said with a mischievous grin on his face. "Hey man, your grandfather looks tall and is black as coal. I never saw a better dressed black man in my life. And what are those brown things around his ankles over those shiny black boots?"

"Spats, don't you know anything?" I said teasing him. But I had asked the same question of my father who told me what they were.

My Grandpa Clarence had dark chestnut colored skin, just like mine. To me, he looked tall for a black man. My mother said he was almost six-foot-four inches. He stood proud like an African prince in my imagination. His nose was wide and his lips were thick. In my mind he was a beautiful black man, something I would never say aloud about any man. Grandpa's face looked like mine. We had the same high cheek bones. And yes, he had a big head like mine.

His large rough looking hands had long fingers. They could've been hands of an African warrior, but grandpa's hands were those of a farmer. Grandpa rested his left hand on the on the high round backed chair, which grandma was sitting on. Grandpa's eyes were bright, like freshly buffed black pearls. A golden chain hung from one of the pockets of his chestnut colored leather vest. Mama told me he had pocket watches, one of which hung from his buttoned vest pocket.

He wore the whitest long-sleeved starched shirt. There were cuff links that appeared to be dark gemstones. And I imagined a big gold wedding band on his finger, but couldn't be sure. Grandpa looked immaculate and muscular. I wanted to dress like him when I became a man.

Smokey picked up the photo and pointed his finger at my grandma.

"Mercer, your grandma, she looks white."

Grandma Polly was light-skinned brown, almost white. The photo did not show her skin-color accurately. When I first looked at the photo when I was a little boy, I asked my mother who was the white woman in the photo was? She slapped me hard in the face. My mother never answered my question. And I didn't ask it again.

When that same grandma came to visit us, she looked Negro to me. I wasn't sure. She could pass for being white. Grandma Polly had long black hair with silver streaks that ran below her shoulders. Her skin was a milky coffee-color with a tinge of red. And there were some light-brown freckles on her round face.

My grandma noticed me staring at her one day while we sat on the front porch.

"Baby, what can I help you with?" There was no anger in her voice.

I was too scared to ask her my question, *was she white or Negro?* I wondered if Grandma Polly would, like her daughter, hit me and still not answer my question. I was thinking that maybe the apple doesn't fall too far from the tree.

I made sure I was out arm's reach before I asked, "Grandma Polly, are you white or Negro?"

Grandma smiled at me like she'd heard the question many times before. "Mercer baby, I'm colored. I got some Cherokee Indian, Negro, and white blood in me, that's why my skin looks the way it does."

Grandma had Aunt Queen's voice and smile. Auntie's skin-color was darker, but not by much. She was the opposite of her sister in almost every way. We didn't use the word love in my house but I loved them both.

I had no choice but to believe Grandma. She had no reason to lie about it. In fact, Grandma sounded proud of her skin. Did that mean I had Indian and white blood in me? I felt it was already hard enough just being black. I didn't want people to know I was mixed with Indian. And white blood? Anyway, no one would suspect that by looking at me.

"Man, my grandma told me she was Cherokee and Negro." I didn't tell Smokey about the white part. "She was born in Arkansas and moved to Brighton, Tennessee where she got married to my grandfather."

"I didn't know there were any Indians in Arkansas," Smokey said in surprise.

"Smokey, there are Indians all over this country. Damn man, you don't know shit. Indians were here before white and black folks."

"Yeah right," Smokey said like he didn't believe me.

"Boy, you better read a book instead of talking all the damn time. You know my Aunt Queen she always making me read somethin'."

"Man, just look at my Grandma's long hair. When was the last time that you've seen a Negro with hair like that?"

I could tell that Smokey wanted to say something, but didn't. He went back to looking at the photo.

"Mercer, that necklace looks like some of that Indian jewelry I've seen in one of those pictures in *National Geographic* magazines. And that bracelet looks like a piece of bone wrapped around your grandma's wrist."

"Smokey, I need to get that back to my mother's bedroom. She doesn't like it when I go into her room unless she sends me in there for somethin'."

"I wish I had pictures of relatives at my house," Smokey said. I got some cousins down south but I've never seen them. I think they're from my mother's side of the family. I don't even know if I have grandparents, whether they are dead or alive. Mama never talks about them ever. You know my mama; she would rather whoop me than answer my questions." He looked like he wanted to cry. "Mercer, you are so lucky."

Chapter 6

My Aunt Queen saved my sanity when she came to stay with us for awhile when I was about eight-years-old, and stayed with our family until I was about twelve. She taught me how to read and learn things my friends in school didn't know. Aunt Queen had lived in St. Louis before coming to live with us at a Catholic sanitarium there after one of her lungs were removed because of tuberculosis. She was my mother's younger sister by a few years. They didn't favor each other, physically or in attitude. I think she came to Milwaukee because she needed someone like my mother to take care of her.

The right side of her body was caved-in and was scarred dark brown against her very light skin. Auntie made me help her put a foam brace on that fit under what was left of her ribs to her waist on her right side. The look of that wound made me nauseated the few times I helped her put it on. I don't think Auntie needed my help because she seemed proud of that wound. I guess Auntie wanted me to know she was a survivor. I don't think she wanted anyone to pity her as I think back. Aunt Queen coming to live with us was the best thing that ever happened to me.

My six-year-old sister Birdie adored Aunt Queen as much as I did. Smokey managed to come over many times just to talk to her when Auntie was sitting on the porch whether I was sitting with her not. He liked her too because she was different than most Negro adults. Auntie talked, dressed, and had an attitude about life different than anyone we knew. It was hard to believe that my Mama and Auntie were sisters by the way they looked. My mother was dark complexioned and a big boned woman; Aunt Queen was light brown, the lightest Negro I ever knew. She was statuesque, even with the foam rib brace attached to her side. She had gone to college while my mother had only gone to the sixth grade. It was like having two different mothers in the same house which made Birdie and me ecstatic. Auntie wasn't rich but she had money. She gave some to Mama for rent, and even managed to help fix up some things in the house. It was still a horrible house, but it felt better having her in it. Auntie gave Birdie and me allowances for doing chores, just like the white kids I saw on television. It was the first time we got paid for doing anything around our house which now looked better and smelled better. Birdie and I felt like we had responsibilities for the first time. When Aunt Queen moved years later, we still did our chores without allowances.

"Mercer, I want you to go down to the corner store and get me a bottle of Coca Cola and a newspaper from the box, and bring my change back." Aunt Queen would send me down the block almost every day for to get a paper.

"Auntie, I buying a newspaper is a waste of good money. I can buy some orange slices or vanilla wafers or a big slice of baloney with that money," I would say to her sometimes.

But then Auntie would make me sit down in our small kitchen because it was the least drafty place in the house and tell me, "Mercer, you need to feed your mind besides your belly," she would say. I can remember sitting at that kitchen table reading as my stomach growled. We would talk about news stories of wars in faraway places and discuss civil rights of Negro people. She didn't agree how Negroes were represented in the newspaper. "We aren't all criminals," she would say to herself whenever she came across a story she didn't like.

The best part of reading that newspaper with Auntie was being beside her. She taught me another side of life. And I felt less lonely in the world. When I got older I would buy a newspaper, and usually, candy or cookies or baloney with my own money. I bought the paper out of habit, because it was the easiest thing to read and it gave me some insight into the world around me.

Aunt Queen had lived in places like Harlem, Los Angeles, and St. Louis for short periods of time. She traveled to far off places like Italy, Africa, and France. She showed me photographs of the places she'd been to. My favorite photos were of the Roman Coliseum where gladiators fought tigers and the Eiffel Tower in Paris, where she said she ate French bread with cheeses I couldn't pronounce, along with red wine she drank out of long stemmed wine glasses. Auntie wasn't alone in some of those photos. There were pictures with smiling people of all skin colors and that surprised me. My imagination ran wild as she told me stories about those places. I couldn't wait to grow up so I could see some of the world too.

Smokey was my best friend, and almost everything Aunt Queen told me, I shared with him. He had no one like Aunt Queen at his house to broaden his horizons or make him feel good about himself. Sometimes Smokey would come across the street whenever she sat on the porch in a thick sweater, no matter the weather, when I wasn't home. They would talk about things she would talk to me about. I was jealous because Aunt Queen was my aunt, not his. She straightened me out;

"Mercer, Smokey needs my help more than you do. That's the problem with Negroes; they never want to help children gain some knowledge."

It didn't take me long to understand what she meant. Smokey was like a brother to me, so why shouldn't he know what I knew?

Auntie had been married. She said her husband "vanished" from her life after she went to the sanitarium in St. Louis. The only thing Auntie ever said to me about him was that "he had been in the military." Auntie had not lost her beauty or her mind in her illness, even though bronchitis and pneumonia threatened her well being all the time. *It made me angry to know that a man could not want to be with my Auntie, she was the toughest woman I knew next to my mother.*

I had never known anyone black that had traveled out of the country. That intrigued me. *If a country girl from Brighton Tennessee could travel the world, then I could travel it too.* I was in awe of Aunt Queen. She never worked with her hands, even back on the farm in Brighton Tennessee.

"Queen didn't have a strong constitution for working the fields" my mother would say. I never quite knew what that meant. But Aunt Queen would laugh out loud whenever Mama said it. Auntie was the one to go to school while her five siblings worked the field with their father. It helped that Auntie was light skinned like her mother. Light skinned Negroes had a better chance of getting an education in the South and moving forward in life.

I never wanted to live down South. And I'll probably never go down there, especially if my father has anything to say about it. "Boy, you too goddamn proud, them crackers down there would love to kill a colored boy like you."

I kind of knew that was true, after all, since Auntie made me read the newspapers. But I had always been painfully aware of how the color of my skin offended some white people up North every time I went outside the neighborhood; almost as soon as I stepped out of my predominately black neighborhood and ventured into one that was not, I had to be careful. What I most disliked about this segregated city was that white people had the freedom to go anywhere they wanted to go but black people did not have those same freedoms of movement.

Aunt Queen and I spent a lot of time in the kitchen, the warmest place in the house during the daytime. I made sure the dehumidifier was running in the kitchen and at night in her bedroom. The windows were tightly shut. Until she got better her bedroom and most of house smelt like menthol rubs. I liked those smells a lot better than the *Camel* cigarette smoke that used to hover in the air when my mother and father chain smoked in the house. Mama had almost quit smoking when Auntie lived with us. But the minute she was gone, my mother began smoking heavily again.

Aunt Queen was the only Catholic in our family. Auntie had rosary beads, and when she was down about something, she would close her eyes and rub them and kiss the silver cross. She would then come out of her little trance and be in good spirits. She never complained about anything in my presence. With her problems, why should I whine about anything?

Even after she moved a few blocks from us when I went to junior high, I kept reading newspapers to make me more knowledgeable about the world than my fellow classmates. My teachers were surprised that I just wasn't another ignorant "colored boy." I wouldn't let teachers treat me like one either. I guess my father was right, my "mouth was too goddamned big."

Whenever I visited Auntie she would give me a book or two she wanted me to read. I still didn't like reading more than what was required for school, which wasn't that much. But Aunt Queen would give me money to read novels by James Baldwin, Ralph Ellison, Zora

Neale Hurston, Richard Wright, and poems by Countee Cullen and Langston Hughes. Through those writings I learned about racism, segregation, and injustices in this country, I found the compassion for humanity in the characters in the books, as if I was one of them: and love of self that shaped the way I felt about myself. I could be everywhere and anyone in my imagination by reading.

Aunt Queen always said that "knowledge is power." She once said to me, "Mercer Bevenue, maybe you could be President." Auntie had high expectations for me. I remember not saying anything, it was a comment usually reserved for white parents to their children, not a black boy like me. But I felt deep down inside that Aunt Queen knew there would never be a Negro president in our lifetime.

Chapter 7

The warm breeze brushed over me gently as I sat alone on my front porch. It would be my last few moments of freedom, since I was my mother's *slave* for this Saturday morning. Soon I would have to get my *Red Flyer* wagon out of the basement to go to the welfare food depot. There were times when I was young that I would rather go hungry than to be seen hauling welfare food in that wagon.

"Mercer, go to the toilet before we go to the food depot. We're not stoppin' by Queen's place today. And make sure you put some newspaper in the bottom of that wagon after you bring it out the basement. I don't want none of that dirt and rust on them groceries. And don't forget to get those brown paper bags off the kitchen table when you come out the bathroom."

"Yes, ma'am," I said,   but thought, *damn! Mama, I'm too old for you to tell me to use the toilet.* That's what I wanted to say. Even thought I did have to go to the bathroom. I just didn't want mama to remind me to take a piss like I was a little boy.

Going to the food depot always hung like a dark cloud over me, no matter the weather. On this early Saturday morning the sunshine was warm and the scent of dewy grass was in the air. In spite of that, I still felt lousy. It was a perfect day to do something, anything but going to the welfare depot. It was the first great day of spring, and I was disappointed I couldn't go to the park or the playground.

My head beat like a drum whenever I had to drag that wagon to the Department of Family Services. It was six blocks from my house, yet it seemed like miles away. I liked to go early to the depot, so did my mother. I didn't want anyone to see me cart welfare food boxes in my wagon. I didn't like people sticking up their noses at me and my mother. People looked at us like we were beggars. Yet Mama always held her head high as we walked those blocks to the warehouse, and she urged me to do the same.

I was ashamed to be on welfare, but Mama looked at it as a godsend.

Mama once said to me, "Mercer, those same damn people snubbing their noses up at us, probably don't have a pot to piss in, just like us. I betcha if I offered them a carton of commodities cheese, they'd take it. We're not stealing anything. We got to do what we got to do, to put food on the table. Baby, there are people worse off than us. You need to learn somethin', so you can get a big money job, so you don't have to feed yourself this way."

I knew Mama was right about people being worse off than us. I saw some of them every day in my neighborhood, like Smokey. He ate at my house, more often than my father liked, but my mama would not turn away a hungry child. We never had a lot to eat, but it was sometimes more food than what Smokey had at his house. There were always a couple of bushels in our back hallway or pantry. So whenever Smokey came by to eat, mama would make him take home a big brown bag full of potatoes for his family.

Smokey had pride and an empty stomach at times, but he would never ask for food. My mother often said that "pride don't feed an empty stomach". She knew that if Smokey was hungry, so were his sisters and brothers. He knew not to refuse my mother's offer, because that would be impolite. And Smokey knew his family needed the potatoes. I loved my mother for caring about my friend.

There was very little laughter in my house. My mother seldom joked with us. My sister and I didn't laugh out loud in front of my mother or father. When I watched television shows like, *Leave it to Beaver* or *The Brady Bunch,* those families were always having fun, joking and laughing. They were not like the families I knew. There was nothing to laugh about the way we were living. The fathers on television had good paying jobs and the mothers stayed home to cook plenty of food that the children didn't have to eat if they didn't want to. And the white kids on those shows had clean clothes for every day of the week. Those white kids seem to have no worries. I thought, *man, it must be nice to be white.* I laughed at what life offered me and so the only way to cope was to have a sense of humor.

My mother never seemed to express much happiness either: always worried about this and that. I wanted to grow up and make her happy, take her away from the ugliness of this city, especially our ugly house: The furniture was worn and raggedy. The walls were lemon colored, which had faded to a dull white. The cracks on those once yellow walls looked like veins on an old white lady's legs. The water from the faucets ran rust colored at times. And the plumbing growled like hungry dogs protecting their food. The roaches were so bold that every time I opened the refrigerator, they were right there looking for a handout. I once saw a movie called *The Fall of the House of Usher,* where the main character, Vincent Price, went mad inside of his dark mansion. I considered old Vincent would also have had a rough time staying sane in my little house of horrors.

My mama would sit on the porch with me whenever she could. We wouldn't talk much, but outside the house, I enjoyed watching the world go by on that porch with my mother. I felt free to dream about being somebody and making Mama proud of me. I always wondered what my mother thought as we sat together on our front porch.

"Mercer, we not gonna stop at Aunt Queen's today."

"Why not," I said softly. Mama was always touchy about children questioning her decisions.

But Mama gave me a break today and said "Queen got to do something at St. Boniface this morning."

Auntie's upper flat was about two blocks from the welfare place and we would pass her place on the way there.

When we did stop by, Aunt Queen would serve coffee or tea in a cup on a saucer. The dishware was China, colorful and expensive looking. If it was cold outside, Aunt Queen would make me a big mug of hot cocoa made with *Hershey's* chocolate syrup and real milk, not powdered milk that had to be mixed with water. We had only powdered milk at our house. The real milk cocoa always tasted rich, like if gold had a taste, it would be chocolate. If it was warm outside like today, Auntie would give me a big cold bottle of *Orange Crush* soda, which I would savor (Aunt Queen taught me that word) until the last drop. Me, and my sister Birdie had only *Kool-Aid* at our house, if there was enough sugar. Only adults drank soda in my house.

"Queen, why you got to break-out this fancy assed shit every time I come over here, just to give me a damn cup of coffee?" my mother would say.

"Royal, I'm just trying to bring a little culture to your big country butt," Aunt Queen would tease.

They would both laugh and playfully argue with each other, like they were little girls. It was great to hear my mother laugh. They sounded like friends, going back and forth with words, and enjoying each other's company. Hearing their laughter reminded me of whenever I was with Smokey.

Aunt Queen made sure that we talked about school. She stressed to me that getting an education was the best way to leave a bad life behind. And she managed to always slip a few dollars in my pocket while my mother wasn't looking.

But today we weren't stopping to see Aunt Queen. No, today I had to slave my whole morning away, dragging welfare groceries in that damn wagon.

I was tall, taller than most males that I knew, even at thirteen years old. I was embarrassed pulling that damn red wagon down the street behind my mama. The *Red Flyer* was supposed to be a toy, a toy that I got for Christmas when I was eight-years-old. Now it turned out to be the car for the house and I was the motor. Stuff I couldn't carry in my arms would be loaded in the wagon. I was allergic to that wagon, because every time I touched its handle, my head would ache.

The wagon was loaded down with gray boxes of oatmeal, powdered eggs and milk after leaving the food warehouse. There was peanut butter that looked like cans of paint in addition to. And long cartons of processed cheese, spam, and huge bags of pinto and navy beans that could feed an army. It was heavy to drag that wagon down the cracked sidewalks. I was afraid that the load would tip over if I didn't concentrate on what I was doing. I thought: *At least there is no one on the street to see my mother and me with a wagon load of welfare food.*

My thoughts were interrupted by a voice, a voice that I recognized, but didn't want to hear. It seemed to come from out of nowhere.

"Hello Mrs. Bevenue. Heeeey Mercer." Trina Dobbs' loud, sweet voice came from the opposite side of the street.

"Hello Pumpkin. How you doin' pretty girl? Why are you out so early in the mornin'?" My mother asked Trina. Most people called her Pumpkin.

"I'm just going to Hog Hoffmann, uh, I mean, Mr. Hoffmann's store for my mama before all the neck-bones is gone. Mama said get to the store early 'cause Mr. Hoffmann give all the meaty ones away," answered Pumpkin.

Hog Hoffmann had jowls like a pig and a pink bulbous nose. He was a grocer like Mr. Ziegler, but his corner store was bigger and had a small butchery in the rear. Hoffmann was tall and wide. He looked sloppy, and his white apron was always splattered with animal blood and flecks of bones. He looked menacing, especially with a cleaver in his hand. But he was generous when it came to giving out the cuts of meats, scraps that white people didn't eat, like neck bones, ham hocks, and chitterlings.

Smokey didn't like Hog Hoffmann at all, and it wasn't because of Hoffmann's appearance. Hoffmann seemed okay to me. But if Smokey didn't like him, I shouldn't either.

Pumpkin was plump and curvy. Her lips were luscious and her toast colored skin was soft like cotton. I used to take her to dances at the YMCA and house parties. We would slow dance so close that it felt like we were one person. I would walk her home in the darkness, and we would kiss every few feet as we walked down the sidewalk. Pumpkin would talk nonstop if we stopped kissing. She was clingy, but I sure loved the way Pumpkin smelled.

Next to Smokey Pumpkin was my closest friend, and she was closer to me in the best way.

I desired Phoebe Westbrook, but I liked most girls that I spent time with. Phoebe looked perfect, but she was Smokey's girlfriend.

Besides I had too much pride to show my feelings for her. Smokey and Phoebe was a good match because they were both good looking.

I could talk to Pumpkin about anything, just like I did with Smokey. They never betrayed my confidence. Nor did I say anything they didn't want other people to know, even them.

Pumpkin wanted to be more than friends with me. She would flirt with other boys to make me jealous. I wanted her to like someone else. She was too *clingy*. And I didn't like that feeling. But I loved Pumpkin's body, she was soft, and she smelled good, like fresh baby powder. And apparently she loved mine: all we did together, touch, kiss, and get turned on. It felt good to be with her, but there had to be more for me.

"Pumpkin, baby, me and Mercer gonna go to the Hay Farmer's Market. You want to go with us after you get them neck bones from Mr. Hoffmann? I know it's about a block out of your way, but I ain't talked to you in awhile. We'll wait for you here," said Mama.

Pumpkin didn't hesitate to answer her. "Oh, yessss Mrs. Bevenue, I'd looove to go with y'all to the market," She said in a voice so sugary like maple syrup. I loved that voice.

Mama, what the hell, you say anything about goin' to the Hay Market. I'd been dragging this wagon of welfare food all over this raggedy assed neighborhood. This must be what a slave felt like lugging bales of cotton all over the plantation. I'm hungry. I got a headache that is bound to pound more, now that Pumpkin will be with us. They are going to running their goddamn mouths all way to the market. Damn, this day can't get any worse.

"Come on Mama, you and Pumpkin going to do more talking than shoppin'. Why don't I just roll the wagon home and put this stuff away?"

"Yeah Mercer, you could do that, but then you'd have to come back with the wagon market to pick us up to load up groceries again. So, make up your mind what you want to do."

I turned my head away from Mama to hide my rolling eyes and pouting lips.

Pumpkin met us in the middle of the block. She had two large bundles of neck bones wrapped in brown butcher paper, which she put in the wagon without asking if she could. Her plump lips never stopped jabbering all the way to the market. She and my Mama talked so fast on the way. I couldn't understand what the hell they were talking about half the time. In the meantime, they completely ignored me.

When we reached the farmer's market, Mama told me to wait on the corner while she and Pumpkin went into the maze of people in the coverless roof marketplace. I was hoping that they'd never find their way out.

"Mercer, be sure to watch my packages of neck bones," Pumpkin said, too sweetly for my taste.

I wanted to say, *why don't stick them neck bones down your big assed drawers?* But I didn't say anything because Mama was nearby.

"Mercer, didn't you hear what Pumpkin said? Make room in that wagon for more stuff. Keep Pumpkin's neck bones out the sun so they don't spoil. We're goin' to be back in a minute or two. That meat will be okay," Mama said. *A minute or two, I knew that was a big lie.*

"Yes, Ma'am," I mumbled.

I felt like a damn fool with a full wagon of welfare groceries, which should have been loaded into the back of a station wagon. On the other hand, I was glad that Mama left me on the corner to guard the food because I didn't want to talk to any of them giggling hens.

Eventually, Mama and Pumpkin came out of the market with brown bags of red and green tomatoes, bright green bundles of mustard, collard, and turnip greens, and a couple of gray cartons of eggs Mama put them in some brown paper bags which we had brought with us. She would carry those eggs in her arms so they wouldn't get broken while I pulled the wagon.

Well, at least I'm goin' to eat good when I get home.

I wanted Mama to ditch Pumpkin, so we could keep them neck bones, but Mama wouldn't think of doing that. Pumpkin was smiling and chattering. I didn't think they would ever stop yammering the whole time they were together. She and Mama piled all those groceries in the wagon. I thought, *now these women thank I'm a damn mule. Mama, we might as well eat some of this food right here, 'cause I can't drag no more shit in this goddamn wagon.*

Pumpkin stood next to me as Mama arranged some bags. Pumpkin was rubbing her shoulder against mine. I could smell the baby powder on her body, but I was too tired to get excited.

"Thank you so much, Pumpkin, for coming to the market with us. It was so nice to talk to you honey," Mama said.

"Yes, and it was nice talking to you too, Mrs. Bevenue. I loved being with y'all this mornin', especially since I don't get to talk to Mercer much anymore. I'll tell my Mama you said hello," said Pumpkin.

"Well, baby, don't make yourself a stranger, come by the house anytime you want. Ain't that right Mercer?" Mama said sincerely.

"Yeah," I said ever so softly.

Mama scolded me. "Speak up like you got some damn manners."

While Mama was paying attention to me, Pumpkin smacked her lips together like she was giving me an air kiss. I wanted to strangle her.

"Yes, ma'am, she can come to the house anytime she wants," I said, trying to sound as sincere as my mother. I did have a smile on my face.

Mama looked at me like she wanted to slap the hell out of me. But she gave Pumpkin her packages of meat, and sent her on her way home in the opposite direction that we were going.

"Goodbye, Mrs. Bevenue. Seeee you later Mercer," Pumpkin gave me a wink as she turned toward the block to her house.

Chapter 8

"Hey boy smells good as hell out here. watcha Mama cookin'?"

My father was through the screen door before I had a chance to answer him. It was just like him to show up at the house looking for something to eat, after Mama and I had done all the damn work unloading the wagon.

I hadn't seen him since Thursday evening, now it was Saturday morning. He was probably out playing pool or playing cards or drinking whiskey at the bar my Daddy's brother ran on the north side of the city. My Uncle Sye used to let me clean up the place on some Sunday mornings when I didn't go to church. Smokey never went to church, and he was afraid of my uncle. Besides, Uncle Sye wouldn't let him come with me. He used to complain that I didn't do a good job brushing down the four pool tables. But he let me listen to the juke box for free; I loved the sounds of The Temptations, Miracles, and Aretha Franklin. Music was one of the things that made me feel good inside. It was the only thing I had that kept me from being lonely. The music on that juke box sounded a lot better than the scratchy forty-five records I played so often on my little stereo I had at home.

Uncle Sye always carried a gun in a black holster strapped to his waist while he was working in the pool hall. It was in a bad neighborhood, sometimes the customers would get out of hand, like getting into arguments over card or dice games in a large back room with a bar, card tables, and chairs. Uncle Sye was tough, and could be mean towards customers in his place. He looked like a boxer, like Sugar Ray Robinson but with a bald head. He didn't look like my father, but then again, none of my father's four brothers really looked alike. No one messed with my Uncle. I was afraid to ask him if he ever shot somebody, because he always seemed in a bad mood. So, if he hadn't ever shot someone, I didn't want to be the first. I just did what Uncle Sye said to do around the pool hall.

My Uncle was fairly nice to me, and looked tough when his bald head which was usually covered with a black *stingy brim* hat. My Uncle gave me a few bucks almost every time I saw him. And he asked me how good I was getting at sports, something my father didn't ask about. And Daddy seldom gave me spending money. Out of all my father's brothers, I liked Uncle Sye the best.

Like my Daddy, Uncle Sye loved baseball. He was a Cubs fan, and Daddy was a Dodger fan. And anytime one of those teams came to town to play the Braves they would take me to County Stadium. My Dad would buy me peanuts, hot dogs, and soda during the games, so I wouldn't bother them. It worked for me.

On this particular Saturday, I was glad that there was food in the house, because it looked like he had spent a lot of money on new clothes and a pair of shoes. He wore new two-toned brown and white Stacey Adams shoes to accent his chocolate cuffed double pleated slacks. He had on a new brown tweed sport coat with a white shirt buttoned to the top, even though it seemed too warm outside for a tweed coat. He had coal-black processed hair, and looked "cool as a cucumber," as my grandmother use to say. He had fine clothes and shoes in his closet. My sister Birdie, and even my mother, barely had much to speak of when it came to clothes and shoes. I looked at my sneakers with holes in the soles, and faded khaki pants that had seen better days. I felt my threadbare tee shirt, which was once black, but now was the lighter side of gray. It was almost as if I wasn't wearing a shirt at all. Yes, I was glad there was food in the house, because it looked like he had spent all his paycheck on new clothes and shoes.

The aromas of fried green tomatoes, bacon, and coffee drifting out of the kitchen to the porch were making me hungry. I loved the rind of the bacon; I would chew on it like it was gum long after the meal was over. And there were red potatoes that I peeled and sliced for my mother earlier, which she would mix with chopped green peppers and Spanish onions to fry in hot bacon fat. It was usually the moment Smokey would show up. It was like he had caught some of the aromas coming across my front porch and drifting over to his house across the street.

I caught a whiff of my father when he passed me going into the front door. The warm breeze blew across his body smelled of perfume, beer, and cigarette smoke. The odors temporarily interrupted the pleasant fragrances of Mama's cooking. I am sure my mother was going to ask him what he had been up to. However, I'd never known him to tell her.

I once overheard a conversation my Aunt Queen had with my mother when she came by the house:

"Royal, your husband needs to do more around your house. He doesn't seem to do any work in it. I have never seen him cook, clean, or take care of the kids. I babysat Mercer and Birdie all the time I was living with you. And he gambles too much. Royal, I know he's your husband, but what the hell is he good for?"

I bet my mother was asking the same question. That was the first time that I had ever heard my Aunt Queen curse. She had always been so refined, a word that she taught me. I learned what *despise* meant on my own.

My mother, who normally argued with her younger sister all the time, said nothing to defend my father against Aunt Queen's words. I never knew how Mama felt about Daddy all the time I was growing up. It just seemed like it was none of my business. As for my father, I couldn't figure out whether I despised him or loved him, probably a little of both.

Chapter 9

"What you colored boys got in your pockets?" said the freckle faced store clerk as the four of us walked down the aisle towards the exit of the *A&P* grocery store.

I had a *Butterfinger* and a *Three Musketeer* stuffed in each pocket of my dirty khakis. Smokey, Licorice, and Gaddis had candy bars too. But I didn't care what they had. We got caught. Our first attempt at high crime was a bust when we were only nine years old.

"Don't run," said the high-pitched voice behind us.

What thief doesn't run? I thought. Licorice's skinny ass took off like a bat out of hell. He always ran away from trouble. The rest of us didn't, but we should have. I was just a black boy without money for candy. The clerk smelled like baloney as he clamped his boney hands around me and Smokey's arms with him in the middle. We looked like an *Oreo* cookie being rolled down the aisle of the store. I didn't like to be touched by anyone, especially by a white boy. His grip of my arm was a little too tight. Also, I vowed I'd fight anyone, except my Mama, if someone touched me like that again.

The customers were mostly white people with shopping carts full of groceries. *When was the last time I saw my mother with a full cart of groceries?* They parted the way for us down the aisle which smelled like freshly ground *Eight O Clock* coffee that my mother made at home when she could afford it.

My other friend Gaddis, chunky-ass walked in front of us like he didn't have a care in the world. The reason Smokey and me should have run was that Gaddis would have been left behind. He was slow as molasses. Licorice took off the second heard the clerk's voice said," What you colored boys…." He was fast and the scariest-assed friend I had, afraid of his own shadow. In fact, he looked like a *shadow.*

I bet the clerk thought he was a Milwaukee cop arresting the leaders of a 'colored boys shoplifting ring. The *A&P's* store manager was standing outside his office where the clerk explained to him what had happened.

The manager's office was next to the check-out lines. It was Saturday afternoon and the store was full of grocery shoppers. The frowns on the white customers' faces were like we were clumps of crap they just wiped off their shoes. And the black shoppers just shook their heads and frowned in disgust. I was embarrassed and ashamed.

"Harold, take your hands off those boys and get back to stocking those shelves," the manager said to *Baloney Boy* sternly. The clerk looked like he was disappointed that he wasn't going to get credit for the big *arrest.*

Smokey and I wouldn't have been in this mess if it wasn't for Gaddis. But we let it happen without thinking about what a schemer Gaddis was. I was boiling mad, hot as hell that he talked us into this stupid mess earlier: "Man, the grocery store is so crowded on Saturday mornings that nobody will even notice us slipping some candy into our pockets. If we caught, all we got to say is that our parents were shopping in the store and told us to get some candy. It will be so easy to steal some stuff." And we all agreed to that crap since we didn't have any money.

How could the people in the A&P not notice us four raggedy, grimy black boys who smelled like asphalt from the playground? And I didn't see anyone in the store that could be our parents. I felt so stupid the minute I entered the store, but it was too late to turn back in my twelve year old mind.

I knew it was wrong to steal. We went along with Gaddis without thinking about the consequences. My hunger for candy was stronger than my will to do right. I felt like a criminal, and I didn't like myself on that day.

The manager stood in front of us. His height intimidated me, but he didn't put his hands on us, "Empty your pockets," said the man in a quiet manner. It was like he didn't want anyone around us to hear him. I liked him in spite of my situation.

We emptied our pockets. Smokey had a *Mars Bar* and a roll of *Tootsie Rolls.* Gaddis had all four pockets stuffed full of candy. My eyes watered because I was hoping none of the people in the checkout line recognized me. The candy I took out of my pockets had wet lint on the waxy packaging. My heart was pounding, like it was going to burst out of my chest. Smokey was cool and calm, like this situation didn't bother him.

"You boys have money to pay for this candy?" The manager's voice was calm, like he didn't want us to be afraid of him. He was tall and athletic looking with black framed glasses that seem to take up half of the space on his white face.

Smokey and I just bowed our heads when he asked us about money.

Gaddis spoke up right away with pride in his voice. "Yes sir, I got money to pay for my candy," with an emphasis on *my* candy.

My mouth flew open showing the gap in my teeth, but no words came out. I wanted to curse at him, but I knew better to curse in front of an adult. I kept my anger within and save it for when I caught up with him later and fight him. The more I thought about Gaddis the less I wanted to hang with him anymore.

Gaddis pulled out a few dollars from his back pockets, enough to pay for all our candy. He gave the manager took a dollar and put the other bills back in his pocket. The manager and Gaddis walked to an open register to give him change. The man told him, "Don't come back to this store. We don't need your business."

"I don't plan on it," said Gaddis defiantly as he headed toward the exit without looking at us.

Gaddis's fat ass waddled through the exit doors. He went to church services three or four times a week. His father was a deacon in the Pentecostal church on the corner of our block. He knew the *Ten Commandments* better than anyone. I guess technically, he didn't steal any candy. But from that day on I would never trust him again. To me Gaddis was a deceiver, a chunky black devil disguised as a friend.

"I'm going to call your houses and tell your mothers that you stole something from the store," said the manager when he returned from the register. Then I got really scared. I'd rather go to jail than to go home and face my mother.

"What are your names?"

I was anxious to get this over with so I went first.

"My name is Mercer Bevenue," I said not too proudly. And I gave the man my telephone number.

Smokey had been emotionless throughout the situation. But a smirk and a sigh of relief came across his face after I gave my name and number to the manager.

"I don't have a telephone in my house sir," said Smokey. Smokey really didn't have a phone in his house. I don't know if the tall man believed him or not.

I felt so dim. I was the only one in trouble.

I was angry, mainly at myself for being so naïve. If I was going to grow up to be a thief, I was going to learn how to be a good one. But my mother would have a lot to do with whether I grew up at all after this.

"You better get your black ass home fast before I have to come looking for you," said my mother after talking to me on the store phone. I wanted to die after speaking to her. Just lay me out in the meat freezer and forget me.

Once the manager learned that Smokey had no phone, he didn't even ask his name. He just sent us on our *merry* way after escorting us to the exit door, without any last words from him.

Smokey and I walked away hurriedly back to our block after leaving the store. We didn't have a conversation about what just happened. I was too ashamed to speak. And I was worried about what my mother was going to do to me. I should have said like Smokey to the manager, "No sir, I don't have a phone." We both could have walked free like Gaddis the fat devil.

There was no doubt that my mother would whip me when I got home. I had no choice but to accept my fate. It didn't matter if I was influenced by Smokey, Licorice, or Gaddis in stealing the candy. My mother believed in me doing right not wrong, nothing in-between.

I deserved a whooping, not the beating she gave me.

And Aunt Queen wouldn't look at me or talk to me for days after, which was more painful than the beating I got.

After all the pain for trying to steal candy, I didn't want my mother to ever have to beat me like that again. It was like she wanted to kill me, like she didn't like me anymore. I loved my mother but I never looked at her the same way again.

Chapter 10

My always tired mother was asleep in her bedroom. My sister Birdie and I were watching *Gunsmoke* in our living room. It was quiet until someone started banging on the screen door. I got up from the couch to tell whoever was there to quit banging. But before I reached the unlatched door, it flew open. Phoebe and her sister, Ruby, stormed passed me like I wasn't even there without saying a word. They looked like Siamese twins with hunched shoulders. Their pretty heads were not *pretty* at all on this late Friday night. They sat down on our raggedy couch. I could see that their cheeks were red and the once bright eyes looked dull and remote.

Birdie was in a battered chair next to the couch. We both had the same expression on our faces that said, *what's going on?* Phoebe and Roby were waiting for someone. And a few minutes later, that *someone* burst into the house in a fury.

Mrs. Westbrook was hysterical. Her coffee colored face, a shade darker than her daughters, looked blotchy and wet. They were not a good looking family at that moment.

"Where is your mother? She screamed like a banshee.

It wasn't like this was the first time Mrs. Westbrook and her daughters came over on Friday or Saturday nights. Mr. Westbrook usually got drunk two or three times a month on those days. He usually tried to bully his wife and daughters, both physically and verbally according to Phoebe. Mrs. Westbrook was a beautiful woman, not an insolent child, with pretty daughters that adored her. She would sneak the girls out of the house whenever her husband got to be too much for her to handle. Mrs. Westbrook would stay and hour or two. Sometimes overnight.

Mr. Westbrook was a burley and tall man. He was intimidating because of his dark skin and piercing eyes that seemed to have no color. I liked him when he was sober, because he let me walk Phoebe home from church and he let me set on the porch with her. He never let other boys do that with Phoebe. He once hit Smokey in the head with Pabst beer can for stepping their porch. Phoebe told me about it. I wished I had of seen that. I felt Mr. Westbrook was jealous of Smokey being with Phoebe just like I was. It was just a gut feeling.

"It's like living in prison 'cause he is so strict. I can't wait to leave that house," Phoebe revealed to me on a number of occasions. I wanted to do the same, *leave* this place too; but not because of someone in my house.

———————

Maybe something must have happened to Mr. Westbrook because she was so upset, more so than she'd ever been when she dropped bye, I thought.

My mother came out of her bedroom in a floral patterned house dress. She walked the short hall that led to front door fussing about how we were "making too much goddamn noise."

Mama turned left into the room.

"What the hell are you kids …" She stopped in midsentence when she saw company. Before she had a chance to say anything further, Mrs. Westbrook wrapped her arms around my mother. She wept into her chest like a child. Mama didn't like "grown folks acting crazy" in front of her children. She half-dragged Mrs. Westbrook to the bedroom with her shoes scraping on the worn wood floor. I watched the going's on like it was a soap opera on TV, only with black folks.

Phoebe and Ruby cried softly. And I felt sorry for them. I reached out my hand to comfort Phoebe, but she aggressively flinched away from it, like my hand was ablaze. I just wanted to calm her down. She obvious wasn't in the mood to be touched. I was hurt. Phoebe *had* to know I wouldn't hurt her.

"Don't you put your hands on me," Phoebe said in anger. Her words felt like a cold winter wind coming off of Lake Michigan. It was like I had chicken pox or measles or worse, cooties. She made me feel dirty.

Phoebe didn't *flinch* from my hand last Sunday, when she planted kisses on my face like I was a long lost love. I still don't know why she did it. But I was grateful as a fourteen-year-old boy could be. It was the best day I ever had:

Phoebe's creamy brown face and inviting hazel colored eyes made me drool like a fool every time I saw her, and even in my thoughts. Phoebe was one of the prettiest girls in the neighborhood. I liked her a lot, more than I cared to admit. But I knew my dark-brown skin, and not so handsome face, did not make me boyfriend material like Smokey was. I was jealous of Smokey and Phoebe. I avoided being the *third wheel.*

So it was a big surprise when Phoebe said, "Smokey, I broke with Smokey last week." She said this after church at St. Matthew Methodist AME. I felt happy for me, but not necessarily sad for Smokey. Phoebe seemed happy to be rid of my best friend, grinning at me like a Cheshire cat. I thought, she must have gone through the communion line a few times this morning.

Smokey hadn't said anything to me about the break-up. We both had stuff we didn't like to talk about. Who was I kidding, Phoebe was Smokey's girlfriend. And then she wasn't.

It was on a warm day, hot enough to make me sweat. Phoebe had hooked her arm under my left arm, a first for me with her. She did this after our younger sisters ran ahead of us. They wanted to get home to change out of their church clothes and get into their play clothes. The Ruby and Birdie wanted to play outdoors before supper. On Sundays most families on our block ate dinner a couple of hours after church, whether they went to church or not.

Phoebe removed her arm from mine, and placed her soft hand in mine.

"Let's go down the alley today," she said in her tempting voice. I knew her father didn't like his girls walking down any alley. But Phoebe grabbed my arm like it was the rope in the game of tug of war. I gave in to the *game,* and she guided me arm-in-arm down the alley which ran behind our houses. There was overflowing garbage cans and trash bins and odors that must have been offensive. But all I could smell was the lavender coming off of Phoebe's warm body. I was in *heaven.*

I'd known Phoebe since kindergarten. She seldom showed feelings towards anyone, except Smokey sometimes. On that day Phoebe was more outgoing than I'd ever remembered. I liked how I felt going down that dirty alley with her.

When we reached the back of Phoebe's house she pushed me gently against the cement ash bin. The only thing she said was, "my daddy is going to be looking for me soon, so we don't have much time." I was thinking, *time for what?*

I felt stupid. Phoebe took charge of the *time.* She put her arms around my neck and squeezed her body so close it was hard to breathe. Phoebe's luscious lips tasted like sweet peaches as she kissed me on my mouth, like she was warming me up for something. It was working. I was excited. She flicked her tongue into my mouth, and moved it over and around. I put my right hand around the nape of her neck under her lush auburn hair, and pulled her head close. My left hand fondled her right breast. It felt good, but I stopped. Phoebe took her right hand placed hers on top of mine, and pressed it on her breast. It felt so natural, not nasty, as I touched her. We lost track of time kissing and sweating in that filthy alley. We heard her father's voice blast like a bull horn from the front of the house. I was too worked up to be scared of her big black daddy. But Phoebe pushed back from me ever so gently. She fixed her beige blouse and ran her fingers through her hair. And I was glad I didn't leave my hand print on that blouse.

"How do I look Mercer?" she said smiling at me. I said, "you feel fine, Phoebe." We both chuckled.

She walked to the end of the alley after she kissed me on waiting lips. I was in no physical condition to walk anywhere down the alley. I just stood like an idiot at the bin trying to cover up the front of my pants. Phoebe smiled back at me before she turned right out of the alley. *What just happened?* But I've heard people say, *don't look a gift horse in the mouth.* Like I said, it was *the best day I ever had.*

I thought last Sunday was just in my imagination, looking at the Westbrook's forlorn faces.

I backed off after Phoebe's words, and walked through the kitchen to my bedroom at the back of the house. When I crossed the threshold of my room I heard loud words come out my mother's bedroom:

"I cut that black bastard with a butcher knife. I'm wanted to kill him for doing that to my child," said Mrs. Westbrook ranting like a drunken sailor on leave.

I ran out the back door of the house and across the street to Smokey's house. His sister Brenda was sitting on the porch.

"Where is Smokey," I asked her.

"Mercer, you know where he is, you broke ass niggas ain't got no money to go anyplace but the playground," she said like I was bothering her. That probably meant that Smokey hadn't been knifed by Mrs. Westbrook. I felt better.

Brenda was right about us black boys being broke. There were no jobs for us in this city. Most of the little jobs, like at grocery stores or clean up around businesses went to white boys. places Columbia Park was the only playground that kept the pole lights on until midnight. I ran down the block past Phoebe's house. Their burgundy colored Oldsmobile was gone.

Oh shit, Mr. Westbrook wants to kill Smokey too. He hates Smokey. Phoebe had told me a long time ago her father had a gun and a rifle he brought home from the Army. She showed the gun to me one day on her porch. Her father was out of the house. She said it was a German Luger. I was impressed but afraid to touch it.

All the time I was running to the park, I was thinking, *what if Smokey isn't there?* The park was only four blocks away from my house. And when I got there…

Chapter 11

I'd known the Pasquale family since I was a baby boy. Tony Pasquale and I were born on the same day, only hours apart in Deaconess Hospital on Wisconsin Ave. There were seven children in the Pasquale family, Tony was the youngest. His parents were from Italy. His grandmother lived with them but spoke little English. As a result, the family spoke Italian whenever I came to their house.

Yet, his father spoke English well and his mother spoke the language better. The grandmother spoke in gestures with her hands, rather than words. She seemed to like me. Every time I came by she would pat the seat of dining chair next to her with her wrinkled hand for me to sit there. She talked to me in Italian, and I played like I understood what she was saying. Ironically, Grandma seemed lonely in a house full of family.

The Pasquale's had one of the better rundown houses on the block, white with blue trim on the eaves. What made the house nicer than the other houses was that it had a nice lawn and a white picketed fenced-in backyard. They were the last white family on the block.

I used to sit on their front porch usually with Tony and Frankie, but Smokey was not welcome on the porch. Smokey didn't care. Smokey didn't like being around white people. The family treated me like the color of my skin didn't matter, plus I was one of the few black boys that would play with Tony growing up.

I loved eating homemade pizza, Italian sausage and lasagna at their long kitchen table with their family. The inside of the house always smelled of garlic, oregano, and yeast. My mouth would water before I sat down to eat at their long wooden kitchen table. The fragrances smelled so good in that house that I wanted to bite the air. The tastes of olive oil, yeasty bread, Italian sausages, savory tomato sauce, and cheese I couldn't pronounce on top of pizza, would linger with me for days after eating that food. Next to my mother, Mama Pasquale was the best cook I knew.

I listened to the Italian spoken at the table like I was having a meal in a different country. There was some English spoken at the table while we ate, but talked Italian whenever they didn't want me to know what they were talking about. When I was a boy I didn't care what they talked about at their table as long as there was more food to eat. But I felt a little self-conscious that they were talking maybe in Italian about me.

There came a day when eating at the Pasquale's wouldn't be an option anymore: On my front porch on a warm Sunday afternoon, Tony was bragging about his big brother's basketball skills to Smokey.

"Frankie is tight," said Tony trying to sound like a black boy using slang. It just didn't sound right; there was no *soul* in his voice like the black boys on the block he heard talking slang. It just wasn't in Tony's nature to sound like those boys.

Smokey called Frankie, "Franco," and Tony, "Antonio," because it irritated them. He and Tony argued all the time growing up. They seemed to like each other, which I never understood. When Frankie and I were with them we mostly ignored them.

"Antonio, I bet you a dollar that Mercer could beat Franco on the Square, I'd play him myself if I had a better pair of good tennis shoes," said Smokey. He didn't have a dollar, nor did I. And my shoes were almost as raggedy as Smokey's.

"Smokey, don't be volunteering me for shit, that bet is between you and Tony. I just want to sit here with Frankie, not play any basketball today," I said. It was like Smokey and Tony didn't hear what I said and kept on talking crap with each other.

"Antonio, Mercer can beat Franco with one hand behind his back 'cause your brother is a raggedy assed scrub," said Smokey.

"I'll take that bet," said Tony without asking Frankie.

"Stupid-assed bet. Mercer is gonna kick Franco's ass on the court," said Smokey.

Smokey and Tony were boys that didn't want to commit to personal challenges, all they did was talk shit but no action. Mostly they just liked to rant with each other about this and that. In this case, they were like promoters of a basketball game between two players, me and Frankie. I hated the idea of being used. I wanted to be in charge of my own fate like getting caught shoplifting candy at a grocery store with some friends.

"Hey Smokey, I don't want you to lose your money betting on Mercer. Man, he's still in junior high and I'm on the high school varsity. The game wouldn't be fair," said Frankie in a cocky tone.

"Come on Mercer, play him so you can shut his punk-ass up," said Smokey.

"Why don't you take your country ass across the street and find some shoes, then you can play Frankie" I said to Smokey.

"Mercer, you know the only shoes I got are on my feet, and too damn raggedy to play on that asphalt on the Square," Smokey said.

I just rolled my eyes at him. I wanted to take-off my crappy tennis shoes and throw it at him, to show Smokey that my shoes were just as raggedy as his were.

"Yeah Smokey, I don't want to waste my time playing you or Mercy," said Frankie.

Frankie pissed me off with his cockiness. I looked at his pristine white *Chuck Taylor.* Those tennis shoes looked like they'd never been on any playground. I didn't want to play him. But I couldn't let him think that he was better than me at basketball.

"If you think you're up to it Frankie, let's go over to the Square and play the best out of three games to seven points. If you are as good as you say are, then it shouldn't take you long to whoop my ass," I said.

"Wow Mercer, I didn't think you had the guts to play me. I give you credit for that," said Frankie like he was trying to psyche me out.

"No Frankie, I give *you* credit for playing me."

I went into the house to get my basketball and when I came out of the screen door Smokey grabbed it. He went down the stairs to the sidewalk. He started dribbling the ball down the block towards the Franklin Square playground three blocks away. The rest of us walked behind him.

Once we made it to the basketball courts and started the games, Frankie insisted that I take the ball out of bounds. Why did he want to do that? I was five-feet-ten and Frankie was a couple of inches taller, but I was heavier by more than a few pounds. Frankie went to a private all boys Catholic high school downtown. Tony was going there in the fall. And Smokey and I were going to the huge public schools in the city which we could see from the playground.

Frankie gave me the ball. I dribbled past him and made a layup. It was too easy. Frankie stood there like a statue. He just didn't expect me to be fast. Then I bullied him on the court, pushing and elbowing him; all things done to me when I first started playing on this asphalt. Frankie was soft, both physically and emotionally. His body felt mushy like a sponge, even though he looked lean. I punished him by playing defense so he couldn't get a shot off. No one called fouls while playing on the playground. And I blocked him out from getting rebounds. I barely broke a sweat. But Frankie's face was wet, and his reactions to my movements were slow. This told me that he was not a real *player.* He seemed stunned that I, an eighth grader, was sweeping up the court with him like a broom. His face was twisted and red. He looked angry. Frankie wanted to say something, but he was having trouble breathing on that sun drenched court. I felt good though.

I roughed Frankie up, just like the boys did to me on the playground. It was playground rules, no time outs or calling fouls. Frankie didn't score in the best out of five games we played to seven points. It didn't matter that Frankie was a white boy because I played every kid the same way.

"You nigger bastard," Frankie said when he caught his breath.

"Kick his ass Mercer," Smokey yelled from side court.

If he had said, "Mercer you bastard," his right eye wouldn't have met my fist. I hit him hard with my hand in his right eye. It felt like I hit a doorknob with my knuckles. Now I know why boxers wear gloves. We both groaned like old men getting out of bed in the morning, only Frankie was louder. He stumbled back like a drunk being pushed out of a tavern.

Flecks of our flesh, mixed with sweat, dirt, and blood felt sticky, like strawberry jam on my right hand. I felt queasy. I thought I was going to throw up. Frankie cupped his hands around his ears as he tried to gain his footing. I'd never hit someone so hard before. Maybe he had a headache too.

Frankie had a small gash under his eyebrow and a longer one on his cheekbone. His blood trickled down his cheek with teardrops that looked like pomegranate seeds. The skin around his eye was swelling to a purple and black color. It looked like a plum had an eyelash where his eye used to be. I felt the urge to throw up again. The left side of Frankie's olive colored skin looked handsome; the other side looked the opposite.

I had landed only one punch on Frankie's hard head, and my hand was a swollen, a bleeding brown softball and my fingers looked like Twinkies. It may have been my imagination, but it seemed like a lot of drama to give another kid a black eye, Frankie knew better than to call me a "nigger." I wasn't color blind, but it made me sad that he had crossed the line in our friendship that would never be again.

"Frankie, are you alright," Tony said meekly. Tony had the same olive-brown skin color as his brother, but his face was now beet red. He grabbed my blue sweat cloth from the metal bleachers at the side of the court. He tried to cover his brother's bruised around his eye. I liked having to have a dark cloth when I played on the playground to cover the color of dirty sweat and on occasion, blood. I didn't mind Tony taking the cloth for his brother. He tried to put his arm around his big brother's shoulder, but Frankie brushed it off like he was a fly. The boys turned their backs to me and Smokey as they headed back to the neighborhood. I knew neither one of the boys would ever tell anyone exactly what happened on the playground.

"Hey Tony, where is my dollar?" Smokey said as he ran behind the Pasquale brothers.

Tony turned around and took out a crumpled up dollar bill. He looked like he wanted to throw it at Smokey, but thought better after looking at Frankie's face. He put the bill in Smokey's hand, without muttering a word as he ran to catch up with big brother.

I was hurting too bad to hit Frankie again, as Smokey's suggested I do. I just wanted to get out of the hot sun and soak my hand in cold water, hoping to leave the taste, smells, and punch on the asphalt behind. The taste of grit, dirt, and salt from the sweat hung on my lips when I licked my lips. The tar from the asphalt smelt like a stink bomb exploded. I rolled my fist up in my drenched tee shirt; it looked like my arm was in a sling. I just wanted to leave the playground and the incident between Frankie and me behind.

Smokey and I followed the brothers at a short distance behind to our block. Smokey started dribbling my damn basketball again. I told him to stop; he did. He talked about how he was to spend that dollar I won. I wasn't interested in talking, my hand hurt too much to say anything. He didn't ask how I was doing. It was like he was happy that I hit Frankie. Later, I often wondered if Smokey was jealous of the relationship I had with the white boys.

"Damn, you messed up your hand hitting that punk-assed Franco," Smokey said.

"Is it messed up enough for you to give me the whole dollar?"

"Ah Mercer, you know I would a played Franco if I had some tennis shoes."

I ignored Smokey after his lame excuse for not playing Frankie himself. Beating Frankie in basketball wasn't worth it. I got hurt hitting him, but I had to do it. I thought we were friends. Yet, I think losing him as a friend hurt more than the swollen hand.

The tone in Frankie's voice when he called me that word sounded like the white boys' that called us vulgar names whenever they drove their cars through our neighborhood. They never got out of the cars to confront us, the cowards. I had wondered what kind of game these white kids were always playing with black kids. What was the purpose of that hate towards us? Unfortunately, I got used to the white people trying to intimidate me in believing that I didn't matter.

Chapter 12

Phoebe Westbrook's creamy brown complexion and sultry eyes made boys swoon every time they looked into her beautiful face. I got to see her almost every day growing up, so I should know. Her prominent lips were alluring, and I longed to kiss them. Whenever Phoebe spoke through that perfect mouth, she had the beckoning voice of a woman even at fourteen years old. Her auburn hair was breathtaking, especially since that color of her hair was different from the black girls I knew. I longed to hold her shapely body in my arms, which turned out to be Smokey's job, because he was Phoebe's boyfriend. I was soon to learn that *beauty was only skin deep* when it came to Smokey and Phoebe.

Smokey was too into himself to be with any girl in my opinion. He had basically insinuated that during Easter break, our last semester at Robert Fulton Junior High School. We were sitting on my front porch shivering, more so for Smokey than me. The snow was gone from the landscape but the bold chill of winter was still hanging around.

"Man, I like the freshness of the cold air. It's better than being in stuck in my stale smelling house," I said to Smokey.

"I'm freezing my ass off," said Smokey. He always complained about the weather in all seasons, but winters aggravated him the most. I agreed with him about the winters, I didn't like it either. I couldn't do anything about it except wear more clothing.

"Mercer, let's go to California after we get out of high school. Man, the weather and the girls are warm all the time. Shit, I think I'm good looking enough to get into the movies like Sidney Poitier, I look better than his black ass."

"First off Negro, you don't look that damn good. Secondly, it takes acting skills, which you don't have. I'm not saying you can't be an actor, but you got to have a plan before you get to Hollywood. Did you tell Phoebe about wanting to be a movie star?"

"Nah man, not really. Phoebe said she wanted to be a model, somethin' like that. Anyway, I got more chance to be in the movies, than she does doing that modeling shit. Phoebe is pretty, but black women have a less chance of making it than black men.

"I'm not sure that's right Smokey. I go to the movies all the time and I see Negro women, although most of them are light-skinned, but far more than Negro men," I said.

"Well anyway, I'm better looking than your ugly ass, I got a better chance of being an actor than you do," said Smokey. What he said didn't bother me much because I knew that friends often said things that were cruel to each other. Yet, I sometimes wondered why Smokey was my best friend.

"I don't want to be an actor. You think you can get by on your looks? There are plenty of black people that look better than you. I bet most of them know they couldn't get to the next level in anything without brains and a plan. Your black-ass don't have either. Shit man, how many black folks you see on the movie screen men or women? Not many I bet." I said.

"Mercer, I'm not stupid." He said like he was offended by my words.

I didn't mean to hurt his feelings, okay maybe I did, he hurt mine. Smokey was so wrapped up in himself that he wouldn't notice if he hurt someone's feelings or not.

"Nah, man, I'm just saying if you got big dreams you can't just depend on good looks to get you what you want. You and Phoebe are just alike, thinking that being *pretty* is the only thing you need to get by, that shit doesn't work. What ya'll gonna do if one day you both woke up and were ugly as everybody else?"

"First of all, I'd kill myself. And secondly, I'd kill Phoebe," he said jokingly.

I didn't laugh. It wasn't funny to me. What I heard Smokey say was that *people that didn't look like him, and Phoebe, didn't matter.*

"Man, you know Phoebe is only temporary, I like being with her 'cause she is fine as hell. She doesn't need to know anything other than being with me."

"If you're just using Phoebe, then your funky ass doesn't deserve a girl like her."

"Mercer you just jealous, 'cause you know you'll never get a get a girl like Phoebe."

"Maybe I am jealous of you. I will tell you, we'll no longer be friends if you hurt Phoebe." Smokey said nothing as he got up from his seat and walked down the porch steps and across the street to his house in a huff. I was tired of talking him anyway. We didn't speak for a few days, until Smokey came over to my house after we had ignored each other to sit with me on my porch steps because it was warm outside. He had a slight smile on his face and neither one of us would apologize for the things we said. "You want to go play some basketball at the Square?" It was like nothing happened between us. The subject of Phoebe and Hollywood never came up again in our conversations.

———————

Phoebe's light skin was an obvious beauty in an unattractive community. I liked her a lot, more than I cared to admit. But I knew at an early age that my dark skin and not so handsome face did not make a good match with Phoebe. It wasn't that Phoebe didn't like me, but we knew too much about each other. There was no mystery to our friendship.

In grade school and junior high the teachers always seated Phoebe with the white kids and light skinned Negroes. Smokey sat next to Phoebe which pissed me off because I was jealous. The dark skinned kids sat in the back of the room and I sat in the middle rows with other chestnut colored boys and girls. I felt like a middle child sitting in those classrooms, never getting much attention from the teachers. I was just as smart as anyone in the classroom, but seldom got a chance to prove it. But some of the dark skinned kids in the back of the room were more intelligent than I was, and probably could have even led some of the lessons if given the opportunity to shine. Those teachers made me feel like I didn't belong, but what upset me the most was that Smokey and Phoebe believed that they were better than us black kids because their skin was lighter. They were two of my closest friends growing up, but I will never forget how inferior I felt whenever we were all together at the same time.

———————

Whenever Phoebe's father got drunk, usually two or three times a month, he would beat his wife. It is not what was said directly, but I'd never seen ironing cord welts on a woman's legs and arms before. I know what welts look like and feel like since my mother practiced on my ass many times before. But Mrs. Westbrook was not a badly behaved child; she was a beautiful woman, with two pretty daughters, Phoebe and her younger sister by a couple of years, Ruby, however, those girls never came by our house with any kind of physical scars that I could see.

Mr. Westbrook was burley and an ebony colored man with a violent temper whenever he got drunk. He had been in the Army and ran his household like a drill sergeant according to Phoebe and Ruby; everything had to neat and clean in their house at all times.

"It's like living in a prison, 'cause Daddy is so strict. He never lets us get of the porch to play with the other kids on the block. He even hit Smokey with an almost empty can of Blatz beer when he came to sit on our front steps a couple of days ago," said Phoebe when the last time she came by the house.

I knew Mr. Westbrook threw stuff at boys that came to their porch to talk to their daughters. Yet, he never threw anything at me. It made me wonder why? I guess he thought I was an ugly rooster that his daughters wouldn't be attracted to. I thought, *shit, good looks ain't everything.*

I wasn't feelin' Phoebe's misery when it came to Smokey. He was my best buddy, but he deserved to be hit in the head with a beer can only 'cause he was with Phoebe.

Mrs. Westbrook would sneak out her house with her daughters whenever her husband got drunk. She would come by our house to stay with us for hours or even a day or two. Those were the times that she had been hit with the ironing cord by her husband. Her beige legs and arms looked like fat red worms were wrapped up and down them. My mother would doctor up Mrs. Westbrook as best she could and dry her tears with a damp face towel and listen to her moan about her husband and ask my mother, "What am I going to do?" I don't know if my mother ever answered Mrs. Westbrook's question, but I do know if my father ever hit my mother, he'd be buried somewhere. But my father was not the kind of man to hit my mother.

I didn't like other people coming to our unkempt and messed up house. Our house looked like ugly furniture exploded against the cracked walls with the ugly paint. By others coming by meant I had to give up my bedroom, change the sheets, sweep the floors, and put my dirty clothes down the clothes chute. But I heard a lot about their family, usually eavesdropping on conversations with my mother and Mrs. Westbrook. Since the walls in my house were cardboard thin with cracks, I couldn't help but hear what ugly things were happening in Phoebe's house.

Chapter 13

"Your mudder don't pay bill," Mr. Ziegler said after reading my mother's note and looking into a thick green ledger. He threw the piece of paper that slid across the counter at me, like he wanted me to fetch it. The note read:

> *Mr. Z plese give Mercer the things on this list.*
> *Could you plese see yor way for me to git some things*
> *on accont. I will setle up with you next friday. I need 2*
> *cans of cream corn, 2 paks of orang kool aid, a small*
> *piec of salt pork, a pak of winstons, a box of yello corn*
> *meal and a coke.*
> *Royal*

Mr. Ziegler, most people called him Mr. Z, was a scrawny man with an irritating Jewish accent. I seldom read Mama's notes when I went to the corner stores in the neighborhood. I read it this time because I was hungry, and wanted to know what was for supper. It was the first time that Mr. Z was going to send me home empty-handed.

Mr. Z's small store was a dusty place which smelled of sawdust and damp wood. There was no fresh fruit or vegetable odors in it. He seldom had any anything fresh to sell anyway, except a bushel or two of red and green apples in the fall months. The store was an eyesore on the corner, but it looked better than most of the houses on my block. There were canned and boxed goods in neat rows on tall shelves on both sides of a long aisle. One of the shelves ran in front of the counter and the other was on the far wall at the front door. It would have been easy to take something off the shelves and walk out the door. But Mr. Z knew everyone that came into the store and where they lived.

I could have sworn that there were cans on the shelves that were there from when I was in elementary school. Rows of baloney, salami, cheese, and hog head cheese lined the refrigerated meat case next to the counter. I loved that stuff and it made my mouth water. But I couldn't buy any of it. The food cost twice as much at Mr. Z's, than it did at the A&P supermarket four blocks away. But Mama couldn't put groceries or cigarettes on a tab at the A&P.

Mr. Ziegler had a rat-like face, with cold grey-blue eyes that gave me chills even in summer. He had a pink hooked nose far too big for his face. Black framed eye glasses hung low on his nose, and he never seemed to look through the glass lenses when he was talking to me.

He took out a thick green ledger book from under the scarred counter. He tucked it under his armpit and walked with his back to me towards a sweaty fat white man in a tight blue suit standing at the front window.

"I'm not a dog playin' fetch Mr. Z you don't have to throw stuff at me."

He brushed me off like I wasn't there. I was embarrassed because there were other black people in the store. Mr. Z ignored us all like we didn't matter.

Mr. Z turned his head and said, "Mercer, yur mutter es goin' to hear about diss."

I don't give a damn who you tell, Mama or Jesus Christ, is what I wanted to say. But I thought about the consequences my mother would pay for my outburst. Mr. Z had too much power in the neighborhood. No one messed with the little white man with the corner store.

I wasn't having one of those turn the other cheek moments that Martin Luther King Jr. was always talking about either. I wanted to add another dent to the can of peas that sat on the shelf behind me by hitting Mr. Z in the head with it. I was angry and hungry, and felt little crazy, but not dumb enough to throw a can of peas at Mr. Z.

I didn't know if Mr. Z liked black people or not, but I would never set foot in his store again. Once Mr. Z or the one of the other people in the store told on me to Mama, she would whoop me. She would never let me tell my side of the story. In Mama's eyes children did what they were told and stayed in their place, even though the adults were in the wrong.

I was twelve years-old and I disliked a lot of people. But I never thought one of the them that I would become to dislike would be *Mr.*

Z. I would wonder, *Why a few dollars worth of food meant so much to him, when he had so much?*

On one of my previous visitors, Mr. Z was talking loudly in Yiddish to a man up front. The man cringed as Ziegler gestured with his index finger at the man's large head. I guess the one sided conversation was about money because of the open ledger he was pointing to with his bone white index finger. Mr. Z was wearing a bright white butcher's apron over a long sleeved plaid shirt. It seemed like he wore that shirt everyday no matter the weather over the years that I've known him. I thought it funny that he bought a new car almost every other year, but wouldn't spend money on a new shirt.

He looked over his eye-glasses and pointed at a line in the ledger where the blue suited man could see. The man sweated more as he listened to Mr. Z rant. His voice wasn't as puny as I thought. I didn't know if the man owed Mr. Z money or collected money from people that did. He just seemed jittery listening to Mr. Z. The only words the man said was, "Friday, Herr Ziegler" and hurriedly left the store.

———————

In the winter Smokey and used to always shovel the sidewalks around Mr. Z's store, since we were seven old. We were a team. After clearing snow off the sidewalks around the store and his car, we'd go to Third St., where the businesses were to make some snow shoveling money. We made it easy for people in the neighborhood to get into his store. Mr. Z was generous and never cheated me and Smokey, unlike the white business owners uptown. We could always count on him giving us a few bucks each and some free candy bars. Now after the *note* incident in his store, I didn't know whether I was going to shovel snow around his place again.

People in the neighborhood depended on Mr. Z's corner store. Many black families were in debt to him for food or housing, usually both. He ran a weekly tab on account for people at the store. And he owned houses in the community which he rented out. White people sold their houses to him when they fled in the community in the early sixties.

On the way home from Mr. Z's I thought about a book my Aunt Queen paid me to read. It was called *The Grapes of Wrath* by John Steinbeck. I didn't want to read it. I read it because Aunt Queen gave me five dollars after doing so, and she quizzed me to make sure I did. I remember getting that five dollars and running down to Z's to buy some baloney and *Wonder Bread.* Mr. Ziegler reminded me of those rich California landowners that took advantage of poor people trying to escape *The Dust Bowl* in Oklahoma that I read about in the book. They called them Okies. And all they were trying to do was make a better life in California. These people worked on the land for low wages. The Okies had to pay for rent for the cabins that the landowners owned on their property. And these people had to buy food at the *company store.* The Okies had no choice where to buy goods. I felt that people in our neighborhood were just like the *Okies.* But people like Ziegler had another name for us.

Chapter 14

"I hate that fat-assed white man. And sometimes I hate my Mama for letting that blubbery piece of shit touch her."

Smokey seemed to speaking to himself, rather than to me when he saw Hog Hoffmann the grocer dropping off a couple of shopping bags of groceries at his house. We were sitting on my front porch. We saw the big nosed man knock on the wood door frame at Smokey's house. Smokey's siblings were all outside playing somewhere when his mother let Hog Hoffmann enter into the house.

Hoffmann would bring over groceries, like he was making a delivery so people on the block wouldn't know what he was up to," Smokey told me. "That bastard never really drops shit over to any of the other houses on the block."

I felt bad for Smokey and especially his mother because there were many men that slept with his mother. I spent so much time on my front porch that I saw black and white men come go from their house, usually on Fridays and Saturdays. I recognized most of them. It wasn't hard for me to figure out that Smokey's mother was a prostitute. Of course Smokey knew this too. I knew Hog Hoffmann was delivering more than groceries. There was something my mother told me which always stuck with me, *that a mother would do anything to feed her children.*

I knew at an early age that being black and poor made some people do things that they didn't want to do to survive. And I felt white people figuratively and literally *screwed* us every day. Hog Hoffmann was just one of those predators in the neighborhood. And I promised myself I would never let myself become prey for these people when I became a man.

Chapter 15

"Wait up Mercer."

Damn, the first day that I come to school late, I had to run into Booker Dunbar. I tried to ignore the beast. I grabbed books and a notebook from my locker. I tried to shut my locker, but I didn't move fast enough. Booker was so close that I could smell his sharp breath. He was upon me like a buzzard ready to pick at my flesh.

"Booker, I'm late for class. I don't have time to deal with you right now." *Or ever,* which I wanted to say to him, but he had me cornered.

"Make time niggah. We family need to help each other out, what kind of change you got in your pockets?"

I'd didn't like to think of Booker as *family.* And I'd never admit to anyone that he was my cousin. His clothing smelt sour and musty. He stretched his arm, which looked like a tree branch, against the locker to block me from walking past him.

"Man, you know I never have any goddamn money. So why you want to mess with me?"

"Cause we cousins, man, we supposed to look out for kin. And I know that you and that pretty boy friend of yours, Smokey, made a lot of money shoveling snow for them Jews and Italians uptown." I know them white folks paid you'll good money."

Booker minded everybody's business but his own. I wasn't about to tell him shit about how much money me and Smokey made. I wished Smokey was here now so we could double team his big stinky ass. Junior high graduation was only two weeks away, and I'd figured I needed to handle my own problems without Smokey when we went to high school.

I decided to open my big mouth, knowing it was not a good idea.

"Yeah Booker, you right, those Jews and Italians paid me and Smokey good money. And we earned every goddamn dime. I got some money in my pockets, but I ain't given you shit."

I was hoping that I spoke loud enough for someone to come out and send us on our way. No such luck.

The rapid beat of my heart almost kept me from moving. My words were too much for the unkempt boy. I didn't want to take those words back or fear him. Booker had me cornered and I needed my own space to fight or run. Today was not the day for running. My temper was rising, and from the squinting in Booker's dark eyes, he was getting angry too.

"Don't mess with me Mercer, jus' because we're kin don't mean I won't fuck you up." Booker's voice echoed loudly off of the rows of gray lockers that were on both sides of long and wide hall. I'm thinking, *where is a principal when I need one?*

I felt I was on a bridge with a troll, either pay the toll or be slain by the giant. Booker was not going to get any of my money even though fighting was not a part of my nature. Maybe I was kind of a coward, and the sight of my own blood never appealed to me. My mother was the best at dishing out pain on me whenever I was disobedient. She hit me so hard a few times, that I had trouble figuring out what day it was. Her whooping made me rather timid, and I disliked being that way. When I was younger I tried to hate my mother, but could not. In our house the word love was never mentioned, but Mama was the only person I truly always loved to this day.

I was betting that Booker couldn't hit as hard as my mother. So, fighting Booker would be less painful as my mother's beatings, plus I could hit him back.

I threw my books hard to the floor. They made a loud sound like a door slamming. The noise startled Booker and he stepped back from me. That move gave me some space to move away from the lockers, so the behemoth couldn't pin me against them.

I was almost as tall as him, but only about half as wide. But I could move quicker than the fat boy. A couple of years ago, before he started taking up bullying fulltime, he was a good athlete. He had been agile and powerful the times we played sports. But it seemed the only exercise he got now was beating up kids smaller than him if they didn't give him money. Now he was a lumbering slob in funky smelling clothing. The kids called him Dumbar behind his back. Not because of his size. Booker was sixteen years old, two years older than me. He was only in the eighth grade. The teachers would probably pass him on to the ninth grade, despite of his poor performance in junior high.

I slapped Booker hard across his nose. He did not expect it. Booker was the *slapper,* not the one being slapped. And it felt good to hit him first for a change. He was stunned and I could see that his eyes were watering.

"I am going to kick your ass Mer, Mercer," Booker said in a stutter, like he had a speech impediment. But before he could move on me I heard a door open.

"What is all this commotion outside my classroom door? Mr. Dunbar didn't I send you to the principal's office to serve a detention? Mr. Bevenue, what are you doing out in the hall, when you should be in my classroom.

Mrs. Bobo's voice was the sweetest sound that I'd heard all morning. I wanted to run to her and give her a hug. But I had to act tough in front of Booker. I sneered at him with my sweaty face. He probably thought I had indigestion. He was right, my stomach was churning. *If Smokey could have seen me hit Booker, he'd be so proud.*

"I was just talkin' with my cousin," Booker said in a meek voice.

"I just got to school Mrs. Bobo," I said.

"Mr. Bevenue, you should have said I just arrived at school, not I just got to school." Mrs. Bobo was like my Auntie Queen, very formal, always correcting my speech.

"Yes, ma'am," I replied with a smile on my face.

"Mr. Dunbar, get moving to the office, and I mean now," Mrs. Bobo said sternly.

Booker looked at me with an *evil eye*. He whispered out of earshot of the teacher and said, "This shit ain't over Mercer."

I wasn't worried about Booker Dunbar anymore.

"Mr. Bevenue, get your things together and go to class."

Mrs. Bobo was a teacher you didn't mess with at Fulton. She looked like a model, wiry with the skin the color of hot *Cream of Wheat* cereal. Every kid at school knew she could handle herself. She once thumped me hard in the head with her keys wrapped around her knuckle because I was too loud in the hallway. After all these years I can still feel the pain and the embarrassment. Mrs. Bobo didn't discriminate; boy or girl, big or small, fat or thin, she didn't play games with children. She was a serious force to be reckoned with. And nobody wanted to be embarrassed by a teacher that looked like she did.

I was saved by a beautiful brown angel on that day. The next time I would see Booker I may not be so lucky.

Chapter 16

It was amazing what my mother could do with russet potatoes, green peppers, and onions, fried-up in bacon grease. And the spam she fried crisp in that grease from the coffee can on the stove tasted great. We had potatoes in my house every-which-away, probably three or four times a week. I ate the spam because it was the only meat we had for the week sometimes. It wasn't that I didn't like the canned meat, but eating it always reminded me that my family was on welfare. I promised myself when I'd be able to fend for myself that it would not be on my menu.

It was Friday, almost at dusk, and the sun's reddish glow dipped below the horizon. I waited for Smokey to come across from his house to join me on my porch. He usually showed up around dinner time, especially on Fridays to talk shit and eat whatever my mother cooked. Like me, he was partial to fried potatoes. Junior high graduation was less than two weeks away, so it wasn't like him not to have some trash to talk about someone or thing.

Our refrigerator was often empty; at times it only held a box of Arm & Hammer baking soda. The shelves were often bare. But

Mama always kept a bushel of russet potatoes in the cool hall outside the kitchen door. The potatoes were wrapped in a burlap sack which sat in a wooden basket that usually kept the rodents from getting to them.

Smokey had not been himself all week. It was like a dark cloud sucked up his carefree attitude. I could tell that his mind was full of thoughts, thoughts that he didn't share with me. Whenever we were together lately he was sullen. It wasn't like him not to run his mouth. It was like he was keeping something troubling from me.

I wasn't angry with Smokey for not telling me what was on his mind. After all, I was the one that kept things to myself most of the time. We were not boys anymore, and it was time in our friendship to give each other space to act and think independently. Smokey is my best, friend that he made growing up in the neighborhood bearable. But I was ready to take my thoughts and actions beyond the neighborhood, to find my own way. And I wondered if Smokey was ready to do the same.

By now my stomach was full. And the smells of my mother's cooking still hovered in the air around the porch. It was like I could take a bite out of it and still taste those fried potatoes. There is nothing better than a full belly and warm weather. It bothered me that anger dominated my feelings most of the time. It was the monotony of my life that drove me to anger. Aunt Queen always told me to "work hard and be patient, and good things will come." She said that to me, but it made me angry because I didn't know how to be patient. Aunt

Queen would never tell me anything that would hurt me. She was the only relative that seemed to believe in me. So, I kept my anger inside, fighting the urges to not do stupid things. It was hard to learn how to be patient. And there were times I didn't heed her words. But today the weather and Mama's fried potatoes kept me content.

Smokey looked like a walking shadow under the darkening sky as he lumbered across the street from his house like an old man. His usual long legged stride was missing. There was no bounce in his steps. Normally, before he reached my porch, the first thing out of his mouth would be, "Hey nappy head, what yo' mama cook for supper? I hope its fried potatoes." Smokey loved my mother's fried potatoes more than I did. He plopped down on the porch chair next to mine.

"Mercer, I need your bike now for the mornin' to go to Estabrook." He said it like I was going to give up my bike without question.

"Smokey, you know I don't let anyone use my bike. If I didn't have to go to the welfare food depot with my Mama, I'd be the one riding my bike in the morning, not you. Instead I'll be dragging my wagon all over the place. Why don't you ride that new gray suit you bought for graduation to the park? And don't you have to stay home and babysit your ugly-assed brothers and sisters?"

"Come on Mercer. Can I use your goddamn bike or not? I ain't goin' to mess it up."

I had waited for a comeback about his ugly siblings. Or the teasing about his new suit that that he bought for junior high graduation with his snow shoveling money instead of a bike like I told him to. But

Smokey did not crack a smile, and said nothing about my smart-assed remarks.   He never let me get away with insulting his family in the past. His demeanor was serious, very unlike his personality. My usually happy-go-lucky friend was anything but that. I had never known him to be so sour acting. Smokey had managed to not let living in a house with no father, a mother that was a prostitute, and house full of younger half-siblings affect his good nature. Something else was bothering him.

"Man, my bike is in good shape. I take care of my stuff. I just don't want you to screw it up. That bike is the only thing I own. I just want to be able to use it as long as I can. Smokey, I told you to buy a bike with your snow shoveling money, not that fancy-assed suit. We wouldn't be having this conversation if you'd of listened to me."

"Mercer, I'll take care of your stupid-assed bike. Licorice and Gaddis are goin' too."

"What, you goin' to the park with them crazy-assed guys? Smokey, you know Gaddis is always trying to pull some sneaky crap on somebody. And Licorice ain't too bright. He'll do anything anyone tells him to do. Man, I wouldn't turn my back on 'em. I shouldn't let you use my bike with them going with you."

Smokey looked at me with pleading eyes. It was a pitiful expression, something I had never seen from his face before.

"Mercer, please let me use your bike, I can take care of myself. I really need to get out the house. I got somethin' I need to think about."

I didn't know the word please was in Smokey's vocabulary. He sounded like he was begging. And it made me feel uncomfortable.

"What somethin' you got to think about Smokey?"

"I'll tell you when I get back, just let me use your precious-assed bike."

I went into the house and walked down the short hall to my bedroom, and took the bike which lay against the wall. I had a bad feeling that I couldn't shake. Maybe it was because I couldn't be with my friends in the morning. I convinced myself that I was just being selfish.

I rolled the bike to the screen door where Smokey stood anxiously waiting. I opened the door, and he grabbed the bike from me, before I could change my mind. He said, "Thanks." A word he didn't say much.

Smokey didn't stop to say goodbye as he guided the bike down the porch steps by the handle bars. He jumped on it when he reached the sidewalk and rode it over the curb and up the dirt lawn of his house. He never looked back, even though I said, "Watch yourself."

I felt uneasy as I watched my friend fade from sight around the side of his house. And I didn't like him leaving my porch without him telling me what was on his mind. It would be the last time I would see Smokey alive.

Chapter 17

The biggest dread I ever had was getting ready to go to Smokey's funeral. He was hours away from being put into the ground. In my imagination I could still *see* him running down the dirt lawn of his shabby house to come across the street to my porch. I could *hear* his voice talking to me about basketball, girls, and the city we disliked. Death made Smokey silent and the sound of him was fading away. The last glimpse that I would have of Smokey would be from outside his casket.

The heat of the day was stifling and I had trouble thinking about how I was going to act at the funeral. I stared across at Smokey's house, so desolate. I was incredibly sad and numb.

"Mercer, it's time to go," Mama said from the screen door.

Her somber tone made my lungs heave almost all of the air from them. I felt like my legs would buckle as I slowly lifted out of the porch chair. Smokey's funeral was being held at the Pentecostal church on the corner. It was only a half block away. I wondered if I could walk the distance. I must have looked like one of the old black men that Smokey and I use to make fun of at the park, those with stiff legs and bent bodies. They were so hesitant to lift themselves off the park benches, as if they were in pain. Now I know how they felt.

I wiped my forehead and tried to dry my eyes with a white handkerchief my mother had given me. It seemed that I cried every time I thought about Smokey. My mother had held me tight to her chest on the day Smokey drowned. There was no way I was going to let her hug me like that now, because I would not make it to the funeral if she did.

My father felt black boys shouldn't cry. He thought it showed weakness. And he was no comfort to me as I wept for days in my bedroom. But Smokey was the only one of my friends my father liked. Daddy came in to talk to me the night before the funeral, and, as usual, a one-sided conversation:

"Boy, I betcha when the Holy Rollers start hollerin' and loud praying over Smokey's body, he liable to get up out that casket, run to the graveyard, jump in the hole just to get some peace." He tried to make me smile or laugh. I don't think I smiled or laughed the whole summer of Smokey's death.

"Boy, you been walkin' aroun' this house like the damn world has ended. Dead is dead. And Smokey ain't coming back to life." My Daddy said in a matter of fact tone. He was a *realist* at a time when I didn't know what the word meant. Now I do.

My father would never admit that he missed Smokey too. He came home after work every day since Smokey died to check on me and my sister Birdie. It was a caring gesture that I could never remember him doing before. He and Smokey had something else in common besides their good looks, they didn't like being inside a church. And he wasn't going to the funeral.

"Baby, I can't bear to see Smokey's mama close the casket on her son. It's just too much grief for me, you understan'?" Mama said to me before I left the porch.

I understood. Mama had seen so much grief growing up in the south that I didn't want her heart to ache anymore than it did now. Maybe she could have easily seen me in that box instead of Smokey, probably the reason she wasn't going.

It just felt right for me to do this ritual thing without my family looking on worrying about me. I kind of felt guilty, if only I hadn't loaned Smokey my bike he might still be alive. It was the longest half-block walk I ever took down to the church.

The fragrances of *Lilies of the Valley* perfume and *Old Spice* cologne slapped me in the face when I walked through the wide opened church doors. The smells were sweet and spicy, and swirled in the hot air of the crowded church vestibule.

It was the first time Fulton Junior High had released students for a funeral that I could remember. I thought it was a joke. From where I stood at the back of the church I saw people pause, comment, and pass by Smokey's casket as if he were on exhibit at a museum. And I guess he was, but it just didn't feel right. I thought it was ridiculous that he was dead to begin with.

Most of the kids there could not call him a friend. Some of the adults just glanced at indifferently at Smokey's lifeless body, like they'd seen this *act* before. It was like the students were taking a Friday afternoon field trip and the adults that were present had nothing else to do before lunch. It seemed like people were just glad to get out of school or the house.

The pews were full. I didn't know what to expect Smokey's funeral to be like, but this was surely not it. That was the gloomiest day of my life even though the sun was shining brightly outside, perfect day to play basketball, instead of being here.

Booker Dunbar, the bear of a boy was holding up the procession of fake friends going by Smokey's open casket. Booker's wide backside took up over half the width of the coffin. I imagined his *paws* were going through Smokey's pockets for the last time looking for change. Booker knew how to throw his weight around, even at a funeral.

A burgundy colored runner ran from the back of the church where I stood to Smokey's unadorned casket. Colorful flowers sat on the raised dais in back of it. There were twenty-two pews, eleven on each side that split the church with narrow aisles on the sides and a wider one in the middle. I had counted them a number of times growing up, usually on Saturday mornings. Me, Smokey and sometimes Gaddis, would dust, sweep between the pews and vacuum the aisles and stage. That was the only way Smokey would go inside a church was if somebody paid him. Gaddis' father or mother would pay us a few dollars each, which was more money at one time that we got at home. After that day of the funeral it would be years before I went inside a church.

I didn't see Phoebe, Gaddis or Licorice at the service, but they could have been in attendance. Pumpkin wasn't coming to the funeral. She left it up to me to say her last goodbye to our friend.

Carlotta Martin slid next to the casket and paused as Booker lumbered away from it. She was a fourteen year-old beauty with light green eyes with a tint of brown. Every junior high boy wanted to be her boyfriend. Carlotta only liked boys that were just as pretty as she was. Nobody but Smokey fit that bill. But Smokey and Carlotta liked themselves more than they did each other. Her face looked down on Smokey's closed eyes for a quick moment and moved on. I wondered if those green eyes ever shed a tear for Smokey.

Mrs. Bobo, our math teacher at Fulton junior high, sat in the second pew behind Smokey's mother. She was all prim and proper, with her eye glasses hung low on her perfectly pointed brown nose. She was lean and mean. Smokey and I liked her because she was pretty and tough. Mrs. Bobo liked us too, I could tell, but she wouldn't hesitate to thump us in the head with her knuckles or keys. Even Booker Dunbar didn't mess with her. Mrs. Bobo looked gentle now as she took off her glasses to dab her eyes with a dainty handkerchief.

Smokey's father sat in last pew at the back of the chapel. I had met him twice. The second time was three years earlier when he came from Baton Rouge to see a son he hadn't raised and barely knew. His pew was nearest the exit of the vestibule that led to the street. It seemed clear to me that once the funeral was over he would be out the church doors. He was checking his gold looking watch that shined as he lifted it to his face.

Smokey looked just like him; black wavy hair, caramel colored skin, and bright brown eyes. He was dressed appropriately, the best dressed man in the church with a black suit and tie and bright-white shirt. I guess Smokey did have something in common with his father. He too liked to stand out in a crowd. Smokey's father looked like a man that had better things to do then sit in a hot church for his son's funeral. He also looked like he was going to a formal dinner like the white people I saw in the movies. It was warm and yet, he didn't seem to sweat. He was handsome, but I saw no sadness in his face. He could have been any black man in the church, because no man in that church acted like their son was in that casket.

I was distracted by people gossiping about what happened to Smokey. Some said he slipped off a rock and others whispered to each other that Smokey was pushed into the water. I didn't know what happened, but in the back of my mind I thought that maybe Smokey might have taken a dive in the river from a big rock. I didn't to know what happened to my friend, all I knew was he wasn't coming back. After all, Daddy said "dead is dead."

I started down the burgundy runner to see my friend for the last time. But Sweets Ingram was standing at the casket lurking over its contents. He was anything but *sweet.* He was the tallest boy in our junior high. The dark-skinned boy had a mean disposition, especially on the basketball court. Sweets didn't like to lose on the court or in the classroom. I liked him a lot, so did Smokey. He was the strongest kid I've ever known. But once he looked at Smokey in the casket, he fainted over the body almost knocking the casket off the stand as he fell like a brick across the runner. I got shook-up. It took three men to pick him up and drag him down the middle aisle. I then was afraid to see what Sweets saw.

Smokey's coffin was gray, almost the color of his junior high graduation suit that he wanted more than a new bike. His head looked like a lump of brown sculptured clay with an abundance of nicely combed black hair. My eyes blurred terribly as I hovered over his gray suit all the while dropping tears down on it. Then I knew why Sweets fainted. The face looked nothing like Smokey's. I bent my head closer to his to whisper that *I loved him* in his unhearing ear. If Smokey were still alive, I would never have said those words. Black boys just weren't brought up that way. His chest felt like plaster cast. *So that's what a dead body feels like.* I had to touch him one more time, even if he wasn't real anymore. I lifted my head and hands out of the casket. The tears in my eyes would not stop flowing. As my father's hankie became soaked, I stepped back from that casket to look at Smokey in that sharkskin suit for the last time. I ran up the red runner sobbing all the way out of the church.

My mother told me a few years after Smokey's funeral that Gaddis's parents had paid for the service. And I wondered if it was *guilt money* because Gaddis was involved in Smokey's death.

Chapter 18

It rained buckets on the night of Smokey's death. Thunder and lightning rattled my ramshackle house. And the strong warm wind whistled through it like a sieve. The wind washed some of the sorrow out of the air as I lay in my bed. My room was the only place in the house I could be alone. There I stayed, and didn't want to come out anymore.

I cried so much that my eyes had dried up. The hurt inside was unbearable. And I knew that the pain of losing my best friend would linger within me forever. Neighbors, friends, and relatives kept knocking at the raggedy wood frame of our noisy screen. They wanted to see me mourn, but I refused to let people see my sorrow. Aunt Queen stood watch over my emotions by turning visitors away. Auntie had been through enough tragedy in her life to understand mine.

Smokey felt God was not real to him. But I was raised to have faith that God existed as when I was young man, and not to believe in Him was a sin. I think poor black boys, like me and Smokey, thought that if God was real, that He played favorites. Smokey once told me his feelings about his doubts whether there was a God one day when we sat on my front porch:

"Mercer, just look around us, the crap houses we live in. Negroes ain't got shit. Everybody tells me to go to church and pray to God, and everything gonna get better. I don't want to wait for a place called heaven for my life to get better. It should be better now. I do believe in hell, 'cause we live in it every day. The ones got somethin' are the preachers taking poor people's money when the collection plate is passed around and all them white people."

I wondered about that too. I was too scared for people to know that I didn't believe in God, probably still feel that way to this day. Smokey didn't fear not believing in anything but himself. He didn't need religion. He didn't care what people thought. I didn't want to change him, and he let me be me too. But I couldn't help thinking after all these years whether he prayed for some higher power to save him from drowning? There would never be an answer to that question.

Chapter 19

Junior high school graduation was a blur, but I do remember Principal William's booming voice calling me to the stage. He was a loud, big black man with a barrel chest. And, when he spoke people listened. However, Smokey's death had taken away the joy of getting out of Robert Fulton Jr. High.

I wanted my mother to be proud of me. Mama only went to the sixth grade and Daddy, I think, only went to the fourth. He didn't show up at my graduation. But my Aunt Queen did. Mama was pleased of my accomplishment, but she didn't say so. She seldom smiled, but this day she did. I had not seen her grin for a long time.

Besides Mama, Auntie was the only person that seemed genuinely happy for me. She told me so, after she hugged and kissed me on the cheek after I walked off stage. Aunt Queen wasn't supposed to do that when graduates walked off stage, but Auntie made her own rules. I went to sit with other graduates after releasing myself from Auntie's grasp. I managed a weak smile with watery eyes for my greatest fan growing up.

Principal Williams announced, "Trina Dobbs come and receive your diploma," as I nestled myself amongst the other students. Pumpkin was bubbly as usual. Her pretty chunky body wiggled across stage and accepted her diploma with a wide grin. She was the bright spot in my heart on that night. I enjoyed seeing her pretty plump face blush with happiness.

My mother made me come to the ceremony I cared little about since Smokey had died. I didn't want to go because he wasn't walking across that stage with me. But I did want to be there to see Pumpkin and Sweets Ingram walk. Most of my classmates, many of them I wouldn't not miss in the years after this graduation, all my former classmates wanted to talk about when they saw me at graduation was Smokey's death a week ago. I thought I could talk to them without crying, but the feeling about him was still too raw. Our friendship was like "peanut butter and jelly" as my mother once told us. We were good together. Even Bunker Dunbar, the bully, said, "Mercer, I'm sorry that Smokey's dead, I know ya'll was best friends." And that surprised me that he showed sympathy for me.

And Phoebe Westbrook, Smokey's used to be girlfriend, cried every time she looked at me. Still, I just didn't care. Almost everyone thought that Smokey had gotten her pregnant, but I knew that was a lie. Soon she would go too, dead to me just like Smokey. She was going down South to live with relatives to give birth to a baby that was not Smokey's.

After the ceremony, Mama, Auntie, and Birdie, caught a ride home with Mrs. Westbrook, Phoebe, and her sister in their big brown *Oldsmobile*. Mr. Westbrook did not attend the graduation. I am glad he didn't show his face to see his step-daughter walk across the stage. He didn't deserve to be here. There was room for me to squeeze into the car, but I didn't want to be close to the Westbrook family. I felt numb and wanted to be alone.

I told my mother that "I'd rather walk home." She didn't persuade me to go with them, even though they were going to *George Webb's* to celebrate.

"Mercer, I have something to tell you," Phoebe said before she stepped into the car. "Can I come to your house in the morning?"

I have nothing to talk to you about anymore. I didn't say no she couldn't come. If Phoebe came by the house the next day it wouldn't be at my invitation.

The morning after graduation I sat on my front porch. My stomach felt tight and satisfied from eating a big breakfast. I hadn't eaten much since Smokey's death, and I guess I was trying to make up for it at one meal. Food always made me feel better. I was waiting on the porch hoping Phoebe would not drop by.

The clouds that were once fluffy looking white earlier in the morning, but had turned to a dingy looking mass of grayness, like they could burst with rain at any moment. The wind had shifted from warm to chilly. The weather had made me uncomfortable on my porch, a place that I usually felt good.

While I was looking up at the sky Phoebe seemed to sneak up on me. She was already on the porch.

"Hey Mercer," she said softly.

"What's up Phoebe?"

"Can I sit down next to you Mercer?"

"Just sit your butt down Phoebe. You know you don't have to ask me."

"Mercer, will you still be my friend if I tell you somethin' that I couldn't tell Smokey?"

"You can tell me anything Phoebe, and we'll always be friends, no matter what you say.

"Mercer, I know you think that I led people on that Smokey got me pregnant. But I couldn't tell anyone, especially not you. Smokey and I never had sex. I think he knew something was up with me 'cause I refused to see him for the last couple of weeks. He just didn't understand why. I couldn't tell him that my step-daddy got me pregnant one evening when mama was out of the house. He was drunk. I don't think he knew what he had done until after mama took me to the doctor. I was sick and sad, and she was angry and broken hearted. Remember when my Mama burst into your house while Ruby and I sat in your living room? That was the night I told her that

Smokey wasn't the one got me pregnant, my step Daddy was the one that did." Phoebe cried after telling her story.

My heart felt like it broke again, so soon after Smokey's death listening to Phoebe. I didn't have enough tears left to cry with her. And I didn't know what to say to her. I could do nothing to ease her pain and I couldn't manage to hug her. It felt that it would have been better for her if Smokey had gotten her pregnant instead of her father. Boys get girls pregnant all the time, but fathers just didn't do those things to their daughters. I was so naïve when I was young.

"Mercer, say something."

"What you want me to say Phoebe? I am your friend, I promise, but I can't think of a way to make you feel better. It is your job to be strong to get through this. You know people gonna talk shit about you if they find out. Your daddy was the one put you in this situation. He should be the one that should be ashamed, not you." I said trying to boost her spirits. But I knew it would be a long way back to the beautiful happy girl I had grown up with. She had guilt written on her face. I hid mine.

After Phoebe left the porch I sat there trying to wipe everything that she confessed to me out of my mind. I felt sorry for Phoebe and wondered how she was going to deal with the tragedy of being raped and the loss of Smokey. I was learning that bad things will happen to people close to me. My *job* was to protect myself and try to control my own fate. It was the reason I avoided taking risks, both physically and emotionally. And I also realized that I had no control of what could happen to me in life. The sky cleared and sun shone bright as the temperature began to rise over the landscape of the shabby neighborhood. I started to feel better even with the sadness in my heart.

Chapter 20

I felt insignificant at the beginning of summer, still absorbed in self-pity without Smokey. I mostly sat on my porch eating too many bags of potato chips or pork skins, washing them down with bottles of soda. Every kind of potatoes my mother would cook, from fried to mashed I ate. Meat I wasn't particularly fond of because it reminded me that we were poor, not because it didn't taste good I ate; from pork neck bones, pig's feet, and even spam. That was usually the only kinds of meat we had in our house.

We usually had fried chicken on Sundays but not during the week. Like many poor black families, we had Crowder peas, pinto, Northern or Navy beans to eat with homemade corn bread when there wasn't meat. I was gaining weight and didn't care. All I could imagine was that I wouldn't be fat if Smokey was alive.

Smokey's house looked forlorn as I smacked down on salty snacks while looking across the street. My mother tried to get me to ride my bike or go play basketball at the playground. And do something other than "be a bump on a log" as she would say. Yet, my heart just wasn't in it to do those things that I loved so much. I was paralyzed and didn't want to do anything but be sullen. It was hard to relate to anything but food which made me feel less depressed. I wanted to find a *path* to me again but didn't know how. I had just turned fifteen and didn't feel good about being a year older.

One day my friend, Sweets Ingram, came by my house. I liked Sweets a lot. He was tall and his skin was black as the midnight sky. He was proud of his skin color. Smokey and I were crazy about Sweets. He was our teammate on the junior high basketball team. He was lean and strong. And he was leader in the classroom and on the basketball court. Sweets knew what he wanted and worked hard to make himself important in a world that ignored black boys like us. We were going to the same predominately black high school in the fall.

"Mercer, you gettin' fat," Sweets always spoke what was on his mind; even it hurt someone's feelings. But he was right about my weight, but I just didn't care.

"Man, everybody is wondering where you been for almost a month of summer. The Franklin Square playground league starts next week. All the freshmen coming into North are forming a league. I signed your blubbery black ass up for the team."

"Sweets, why'd you do that? I haven't touched or thought about basketball for over a month. Plus I'm out of shape to play," I said trying to convince my friend, and myself, that I'd be of no use to the team.

"Mercer, don't worry about that shit, I'll get you ready to play ball. Get your fat ass up and quit feeling sorry for yourself. Smokey's gone and I miss him too. But your life ain't over like his but you need to move or else you gonna be dead too. So get up, go in the house and get your basketball."

I didn't move and just hung my head in shame. It really wasn't in my nature to mop about things in life, finding my true self was becoming increasingly difficult. Sweets pulled me by the arms and dragged me out of my porch chair.

"Damn, man, you heavy as hell. I almost cramped my arms pulling your big butt up," Sweets said grinning from ear to ear.

Just then my mother came to the screen door. "I thought I heard talking out here. Hey Sweets, good to see you boy. How's your mama?" she said.

"Hello Mrs. Bevenue, Mama is doin' fine. I'll tell her you asked about her," Sweets said politely.

"It's about time somebody came by here to see Mercer. You need to take him to the playground or do something with him. Mercer is gettin' on my damn nerves, I damn near have to put a lock on the refrigerator, but that wouldn't do any good, Mercer eat all the leftovers," Mama said to Sweets laughing.

I was going to cut my eyes at Mama while she was making fun of me. But I knew better than to do that. All the while Sweets is laughing his ass off, like Mama was Redd Foxx the comedian.

I'm tired of looking at his big butt mopping around this house," Mama said with anger in her voice.

"That's what I've been trying to do Mrs. Bevenue, but Mercer just wants to sit on the porch."

"Mercer, get your ass up," she said with a tone that meant business.

I couldn't say *no* to my mother. If I disobeyed her, she would whoop me in front of Sweets. And I'd rather play basketball than let that happen.

I felt Sweets was smarter than I was, he knew that black boys shouldn't give up because poverty, tragedies, or racism, can cause setbacks in black people's lives. He seemed know that black boy's biggest strength was to believe in self no matter what anyone says or does. I could see that in Sweets he practices what he preached, physically, but most importantly mentally tough moving forward in life. His spirit for being black rubbed off on me.

Chapter 21

My Aunt Queen was the only Negro Catholic I knew. I knew Baptists, Seventh Day Adventist, Jehovah's Witnesses, Methodists, and many Pentecostals. I had no allegiance to any of these religions, especially after Smokey died. Auntie attended St. Boniface church down the block from North Division High School where I was going in the fall. I liked the Catholics the best primarily because they had Fish Fry Fridays during the summer when I was growing up.

Aunt Queen left Brighton, a small farming town outside Memphis, at an early age to live with a cousin in St. Louis. She left behind her parents, four brothers and three sisters to toil on their small farm.

"Why did Aunt Queen leave Brighton?" I once asked my mother. I should have known better to ask.

"She said, "Boy, that ain't known of your damn business. If Queen wants you to know why she left from down south, then she'd tell you."

I adored my Auntie. I loved her as much as I loved her sister, my chestnut colored "big boned" mother, as my father used to say. There were some days I liked Aunt Queen better, she was seldom impatient with me like mama was. But Auntie didn't have children of her own and didn't have to be with me and Birdie all day.

I liked the Friday night fish fry at St. Boniface cafeteria, Aunt Queen volunteer my services before sitting down to eat. I would eat rye bread, perch fish, American and German potato salads, and wash it down with sweet iced tea until I would almost burst. I could never eat that much at home because food at my house was often meager. Smokey would come with me sometimes but he felt uncomfortable around "religious" people. He thought Catholics were strange. My Aunt Queen wasn't *strange.* I never asked Smokey what he meant. The way I looked at it, if Smokey didn't want to eat with Catholics, the more food for me.

But before I could indulge in eating there were two things I had to do. The first thing I had to do was accompany my Aunt to Mass.

Auntie would kneel and make the sign of the cross over her small chest at the beginning of the pews before she entered the church. I would follow her and also kneel and make the sign of the cross over my chest, just like she told me. I thought I couldn't do that since I was not Catholic, but Auntie said to do it so I did.

It was difficult for Aunt Queen to get up after kneeling sometimes. She looked frail to me some days. But she had so much vigor for life that I rarely noticed her movements until we were in church. She would hold my arm as we headed down the middle aisle to her favorite pew on the far right side of the church. It was always cold inside, no matter the weather. There were stained glass windows on both sides that let in very little bright light. It seemed sterile, except for from the fragrance of Auntie's *White Shoulders* perfume.

In our pew, Aunt Queen would rub her rosary beads. I could see her necklace, a silver cross dangle from a chain around her thin light brown neck during service. She taught me how to place my knees on the board in back of the pew in front of us to pray with my eyes closed. Auntie would tap me on the shoulder to rise even though the priest was speaking in Latin. I never asked my aunt if she knew Latin. But there were so many things I never got to ask her growing up.

Auntie once told me, "Mercer, its quiet in *my* church, I can pray and speak to God in peace. The church your mother goes to, those Baptists are too demonstrative and unsophisticated.

"Mercer, do you know what those words mean?"

"Yes ma'am, it means country and wild."

All Auntie could do was laugh loudly.

"Mercer, that's not what those words mean. Look them up in a dictionary, come back and tell me, I'll give you a dollar."

I could always use a dollar.

"I can't hear myself think during the loud chorus, and *holy* shouting from the congregation. Besides I don't like the preacher blurting out passages from the bible, too much of a show for me," Auntie said.

Aunt Queen never told me where or how I should worship, but she gave me a lot to think about at an early age on how I wanted to talk to God.

Aunt Queen was the most educated person I knew. She was the only one of her siblings that made it out of high school. But she had to leave Brighton to do it. Auntie had a two year college degree. She also took night classes to learn Spanish and French. And she found time to work at the Urban League part-time, I don't know exactly what she did, but we would have lunch together sometimes. She wanted me to meet professional Negro people that worked there.

I've read about places like New York, Paris, and Hollywood, but Aunt Queen had been to all of those places and more. She wasn't rich, far from it. But she managed to travel wherever she wanted when she wanted too.

I and other volunteers had to set-up the tables and chairs in the big cafeteria in the St. Boniface school building, which was separate from the church. Even Father Groppi, a priest at the church, pitched in to help.

We had to put table cloths and napkins on the tables: and load each one with bowls of platters of bread, potato salads, coleslaw, and pitchers of iced tea. And once the platters of perch fish was brought out to the tables and Father Groppi would bless the food and people sat down to eat. My job was to replenish the bowls and pitchers while they ate, all the time my mouth was watering. And I was hoping that they wouldn't eat all the food. I thought that would happen all the times I helped out Auntie.

Aunt Queen was in charge of the ten or so volunteers in the kitchen, all of them white. I always thought it was funny that she was in the kitchen. She couldn't cook worth a damn. Auntie was also in charge of collecting money from the people who ate. If people couldn't pay for the food, she would sometimes let them eat for free. It felt good to work for

There were all sorts of people that came to the fish fry; Italians and Germans that lived in the neighborhoods around the church, and black people too.

I always felt good after eating. It wasn't just the food, but it was about serving others that made me feel good even though I never expressed those feelings to Auntie. I didn't know how. Faith was something I believed in, and maybe the only passage that felt strongly about the Golden Rule I learned about in Sunday school, *do unto others as you would have them do unto you.* For me, the beauty in people was what I sought to look at, not their imperfections. And I hoped they would look at me in the same way. I tried to respect people that I disagreed with, and that was often difficult to do, especially if the subject was religion in our conversations. Some people say that *rules are made to be broken,* and I agreed with them. Family, friends, and people I knew that were members of Baptist, Methodist, Seventh Day Adventist and other religions tried to influence me to join one church and not the other. It was like people were trying to force religion on me. It turned me off. Aunt Queen was Catholic, but she always left it up to me whether I wanted to be a Catholic. My mother always thought that going to church would make me a better person. I didn't disagree with her, but I had learned everything I needed to know about religion from Sunday school in the Baptist church. As far as I was concerned, *The Ten Commandments* and *the Golden Rules* was all I needed to know about religion.

Chapter 22

I loved the rhythms, the movements of me and my friends during the summers growing up in the city. The laughter, so loud in the streets and in the alleys of our block seemed to shake the houses when we played outside. My brown skin welcomed the warmth of the sun on it. The sun energized my spirit. And almost always in summers where carefree for poor black kids like me that had nothing better to do than be free in the outdoors.

Some of our parents and other adults would threaten us with belts to keep from playing our *summer music.* Smokey and I loved to play football or stick ball with other black boys in the alley behind his house because it was a asphalted alley, it smelled tar that blackened our tennis shoes. I had an uneven red-bricked alley behind my house. We tried to play on it, but after a few kids hurt themselves, usually tripping over bricks, that's when we stopped playing there. We played in Smokey's alley where injuries would be fewer. The alley seemed to be wider and more out of site of adults. We had to negotiate garbage cans, telephone poles, parked cars, and fences to play our games. It took imagination and skills to maneuver around objects we couldn't move.

It was our *rhythms,* our way of *dancing* in the games we played in summer; and the girls usually played on the sidewalks jumping rope of chalked outlines of four-square in the street. In summers it was easy to be alive and the season was an escape from our sometimes oppressive family lives in our homes.

When the weather was too rainy in summer, Smokey and I would go to the LaVarnway Boys Club usually with other boys from the neighborhood. It cost two dollars to join LaVarnway, but some of the boys didn't have the money, but if you were a member than you could bring a guest in with you. Most of the time we managed to get everyone in to play basketball or shoot pool or swim or just read books. To most of us it was our *home away from home.* There were boys that get along inside the Club. But usually the conflicts were started by that came from other neighborhoods. If there were fighting, it always took place outside off of Club property. If we fought inside the Club we could get out memberships suspended, and most of us didn't want that, especially when the fall and winter months was always around the corner in Wisconsin.

––––––––––

It was the first summer without Smokey by side, and it just didn't feel right. I was blue most of time and I thought too much about him without moving on. My basketball friends, Sweets, Snake, Sleepy, Country and I would walk to most of the parks in the inner-city for pick-up games. It felt weird not having him with us.

I didn't go to church all summer, except on fish fry Fridays with Aunt Queen. It was a summer where church wasn't going to make me feel better. Phoebe was gone to Nashville with her mother and sister to have her baby. And Pumpkin was in summer school taking courses in science and biology. She wanted to be a doctor. We managed to go to a dance or two at the Garfield YMCA. Gaddis had gone down South stay with relatives and go to high school. Licorice was nowhere to be seen that summer and seem to vanish from the neighborhood. The rumor was that his father had made him join the Job Corps along with my cousin, the bully, Booker Dunbar. I didn't miss him because he had never made good on the promise to *whoop my ass.* I was glad that these former friends were not around to remind me of Smokey.

I had plenty of company playing basketball with other boys many days of summer. And the Boys Club always had recreational things that I did get involved in to take up some time. There were too many days that I sat on my porch thinking that I was the loneliest person in the world. Yet, all that walking and playing ball helped me lose weight, though most days after I'd come home from playgrounds, I was too tired to eat. Mama noticed that I was losing weight, but all she would say was, "Damn boy, I'm sure glad that my grocery bill has gone down now that you outta the house running around." My Mama was really a funny woman.

Chapter 23

"Autumn, the year's last, loveliest smile."

William Cullen Bryant

The day was bittersweet, but more *sweet* than *bitter.* I smelled autumn in the crisp October air. Leaves on the trees in Estabrook Park had turned blood orange, yellow, and crimson, a feast for the eyes. There were no cardinals, blue jays, or yellow breasted chickadees playing in the gray sky. Now, the Milwaukee River meandered rapidly downstream and the mist from the spraying water made my nose run and my cheeks prickle. Yet, somehow nature's touch invigorated me. There were no fragrant flowers to smell or colorful bugs to watch anymore. This particular fall day was warmer than usual, a pleasant one even without Smokey here with me. Sadly, it was the last time I would set foot in that beautiful park.

My bike wheels rolled over layered leaves and twigs that covered the grounds like a multi-colored carpet. The crackling sounds of riding over the leafy, woody debris, was the only noise in the fresh air. When the sounds stopped, I knew I was out of the park. I was still a few miles from my drab neighborhood, but time passed. And before I realized it I was in front of my house. It was like my bike pedaled me instead of me pedaling it. I didn't remember the ride to my house, I couldn't recall what or who I saw on the way. The sad cobwebs had been finally cleaned from my head for the first time in months. It was like my feelings of self-pity were in a remote corner of my thoughts. It felt great to think forward again.

I carried my bike up the rickety wooden stairs of my front porch and pulled open the frayed screen door, I rolled the bike to my bedroom and it placed it in front of my closet door. After the morning at the park, I left my thoughts of Smokey somewhere in nature. My spirits had been lifted and I think I was on the way to be me again. Or maybe I was just light headed and tired from pedaling all those miles home.

No one was at my house. My mother, Birdie, and Aunt Queen were shopping on Third Street. They sometimes did that on Saturdays when the weather wasn't bad. I didn't know where my father was. I rarely did. The house was quiet and stuffy. Cigarette smoke dominated the odors in the stale air. It was the time of year with winter approaching, that windows and doors were closed as tight as they could get, which wasn't much considering the draftiness of my old house. It wasn't cool outside and there was no breeze coming through the cracks in the walls.

I went to the front porch and sat down on my favorite chair and looked over at Smokey's house. It no longer pained me to look at it, although my heart still ached for his company.

"Haaaay Mercer, come help us carry some of these bags," Trina Pumpkin Dobbs said to me in that *syrupy* voice.

Pumpkin's voice was both sweet and annoying, because it snuck up on me as I was looking down the block in the opposite direction. It didn't bother me today, and I welcomed the sound of her. And my mother and sister were with Pumpkin, cackling and laughing about something. I had not seen much of Pumpkin after our friend's death since she went to a different high school than me. Her voice reminded me that I had at least one old friend left to talk to.

"Yeah Mercer, come help us carry this stuff," said my sister Birdie loudly. "Help carry these big white drawers Mama bought you." The group of females burst out laughing. There wasn't much that embarrassed me, but talking about underwear in front of friends did.

You all carried that shit eight blocks. A few more steps won't kill ya'll. That's what I wanted to say. But Mama would probably hit me, and I did need them *drawers*.

I grabbed a couple of shopping bags full of things, some light and some heavy, as we headed up the porch through the door. *What is it with women? They can't bear to see a black man relaxing. But damn, those women are strong.* I smiled at them. It had been a long time it seemed that I had *smiled* at anything.

"What you smilin' at Mercer?" Mama said.

The others said almost at the same time, "Yeah Mercer, what you smiling at?"

"I'm just happy I got me some new drawers." I said seriously, but the grin had not left my face.

"Boy, you being a smartass?" Mama said.

"Naw Mama, I'm just glad you bought me somethin'. I hope you bought some food, I'm hungry." I began to go through the bags, but Mama stopped me.

"Boy, get your ass out of them bags." With my mother you never knew if she was serious or not when she spoke. But this time I knew Mama was just messing with me.

"Okay, okay, I'm going to the porch".

Pumpkin must have heard me because she beat me out the door and sat in my chair. It was the most comfortable of the three rickety porch chairs. They were once dining room chairs, and the one I liked had an armrest. I couldn't remember what happened to the fourth one from the set. I wanted to tell her to get out of my chair, but I wanted her company on the porch. It had been a long time since I had sat there with anyone.

Pumpkin had been looking at Smokey's house since she sat down. She usually never stopped talking. Silence was not a part of her character. So, I looked at her round pretty happy face and lips that stayed closed for a change. It was great to be near her with no words spoken by either of us.

But the silence was broken.

"Mercer, I miss him too," Pumpkin spoke to me. And it was all I needed to hear.

Chapter 24

The huge red-bricked building never contributed to the aesthetic beauty of the neighborhood. But the beauty inside that ugly foundation, North Division High School, made all the difference in the world for me moving forward in life. It gave me a start on the kind of person I would become. The predominately black public school was a haven from the onslaught of social ills that threatened many of us poor black kids outside of the school. I thought often that, *Smokey was never going to walk inside those big green doors that fronted North Division.*

I had never been in a school where most of the kids were all the hues of black and brown, just like a Black-eyed pea. I felt so small in stature, like I was painted with the same brush as everyone else. If you weren't competitive in the classroom or sports or some kind of activity at North, you wouldn't get noticed. It was a place like any other public school, only it was a segregated one.

The teachers that taught us were no-nonsense, borderline mean. They stressed the three *Rs*, reading, 'riting, and 'rithmetic. Those teachers reminded me of my Aunt Queen, always harping at me to get a good education. I liked their style, always dressed professionally in front of us, like they were about the business of educating. Most of our teachers were white and strict.

As a freshman I was indifferent to getting to the books like I should have. And my grades slipped. There were too many sports to play and too many girls that got my attention, and I admired them because they were just as smart as some of the boys. I didn't disrespect them for my own selfish reasons. Unfortunately, too many girls didn't return the favor.

Participating in sports took priority over studying during my first year at North. I felt I had no time to open books. I felt only my skills on the basketball court would get me into college. But high school wasn't like junior high, where anybody with *Converse* tennis shoes could play on an intramural basketball team. I didn't think that grades were important. But things were different now, if I didn't have good grades, then I wouldn't get into college in spite of how good my athletic skills were. Auntie was never pleased with my marks. "Mercer, you could do better," she would say when I showed her my report cards. Finally, I did do better for her and me.

There was a group of my classmates that I'd known since kindergarten. They were competitive and aggressive in the classroom, always trying to show up each other in front of the white teachers. I was on the fringe of that group because some of them considered me a *dumb jock*, like I wasn't interested in academics, although I knew I was just as smart as they were. I didn't want to be a part of any *click* anyway. I looked at myself as an independent survivor in charge of my own fate. Anyway, I liked this group of friends. We had a bond that could never be broken in spite of our disagreements.

But it did offend me that after all these years of friendship that they considered me an outsider when we were all in the same 'boat' so to speak. I always thought some of my classmates spent a lot of time trying to prove something to other people rather than themselves. That feeling reminded me of the time I punched Frankie Pasquale in the eye for calling me a "nigger" after losing basketball games to me on the playground. We had grown up together since we were little boys on our block. I never would have believed that this white boy I called a close friend would cancel our friendship by using that word. I guess I never really did 'know' him even though we were so-called friends. I wondered if peers at school thought of me as a "nigger" too just like Frankie.

I believed that Smokey probably would have connected with that click of friends at school. There was always a sense that Smokey thought he was better than me, but he had the attitude that he was better than everybody. I felt heartsick that he would gravitate towards the like-minded kids at school, but that point was moot because Smokey was not alive.

The teachers at North took no guff from students. If we disrespected them or the rules, there would be consequences. I'd rather have a detention or any punishment they would give than for a teacher to call my mother. She was like Aunt Queen in a way. Mama used her fists and Auntie used her words to straighten me out. I liked most of those teachers. They were like our parents in some ways and mete out discipline "under their roof" so to speak.

Chapter 25

"Hell Bevenue, move your fat ass down the court," Coach Vic would bellow at me at basketball practice. It was my sophomore year and I thought my shit didn't stink. I had been a starter on a successful freshmen team. We only lost two games, still Coach wasn't happy about that losing part.

I wanted to back talk Coach. But he was still a Marine in the Korean War mode. I thought he was in the service because he was like a drill sergeant during practice and team were under his command. He would always coach us without a tee-shirt in our cracker box gymnasium. He had bullet holes across his back and abdomen, war injuries. Coach was definitely a man I wasn't going to fuck with. There were also scars on his pale white skin that looked like the welts my mother gave me with the ironing cord when she whooped me when I was younger. Only on my skin you could barely see the marks, but I sure knew they were there.

Sweets, arguably the best player on the team, made the mistake of cursing at another player in practice for messing up a play. Coach

Vic in no uncertain terms told Sweets to run laps around the gym, "I'll tell you when to stop," he said.

"I didn't mess up the play, Snake did, he should be the one running laps," said Sweets

"I'm the coach. I say who runs laps, not you."

"I'm not running for Snake's mess."

"Get the hell out of my gym and don't come back. We don't need you on the team, no matter how good you think you are Sweets."

Sweets' was in shock at being kicked out of the practice. He walked slowly, like a turtle, like he wanted Coach to change his mind before he reached the locker room doors. Instead, Coach berated him as if he was an insolent child. His words walked up the back of Sweets' neck, pushing him faster into the locker room, faster than he wanted to go.

I didn't know what the other players were thinking, but my first thought when Sweets headed to the locker room was, *more playing time and shots for me*. But Sweets was my closest friend now that Smokey was gone; if not for him literally dragging my *fat soul* off my front porch the first summer without Smokey. There was no telling where I'd be without his intervention. I think he saved me from myself. He helped me become a better basketball player, and more importantly, a more confident boy when I didn't believe in myself. But on the basketball court Sweets was a *ball hog,* he never met a shot at the basket he didn't like. In a game a teammate may not touch the ball unless he got a rebound after Sweets missed a shot.

There was no gray area with Coach Vic. It was his way or the highway, He didn't care if you were the so-called *star* of the team or not, every one of us got equal treatment. Coach sounded like my father when he got angry with me and threatened to kick me out of the house. But I knew Mama had my back and would never let that happen. He was like a father to some of the guys on the team that didn't have one. And though he was a white man, I bet Smokey would have liked to have this man in his life. All I know was that I was taking my first steps towards manhood with Coach leading the way.

There were former players that got scholarships or grants because Coach had many connections in the world of college coaches. He made sure most of the players that wanted to go to college went. These guys would scrimmage with us in basketball games in our gym during their breaks from school. And one of the things they all said was that "If Vic didn't holler at you in practice then he didn't care about you." *He must care about me a lot..*

Those former players addressed the Coach by his first name, "Vic", something his current players dared not do. "If you don't give the game all you got, than he was wasting his and your time, as well as your teammates," they told me. I guess that was the first time I began to understand the term *tough love.*

Sweets came back into the gym. We all looked at him like he was crazy after the tongue lashing Coach gave him. But all he did was start running circles around the outsides of the court. No one said anything to Sweets. We stopped to look at him. And Coach started yelling again for us to keep running plays or he'd make all of us run laps too. I was glad that Sweets was back, but I knew I'd never get to my shoot my jump shots as much as I wanted to.

Chapter 26

The scream was blood curdling. It was a surreal event. Whose voice was that inside my head? It sounded so familiar to me? It was close to the end of season basketball game. The sold out gymnasium was hushed. I was in shock, seeing myself over me lying on the hardwood floor in agony. I clutched my right leg with both my hands where my knee cap used to be. It was like my hands met in a divot. The last thing I remember was soaring like a bird trying to block an opposing player's shot at the hoop. It was the first time my father came to see me play. I guess I failed to prove to him I was good at something.

The first words that came out of my mouth as the ambulance attendants wheeled me out of the gym on a stretcher was *will I be able to play again?* I got no answer. But then again, maybe that question had come from my mind only.

It seemed like days before reality set in when I woke up in my hospital bed with the most excruciating pain I've ever had. I thought I was going to die like Smokey. My right leg was in traction. It was disheartening to see a thick plaster cast which ran from the top of my thigh to the bottom of the ankle. It hovered in traction like a plastered drawbridge. Still, I just couldn't believe that this was my body in this hospital bed, the reality hadn't quit sunk in. I cried because of the pain and thought my life was over especially as a basketball player. I felt sorry for myself because of the condition I was in, I thought I might as well be dead as Smokey.

I got slow drips of morphine through a needle and tube from a bag that hung on a metal pole next to my bedside, the drug made me so euphoric, that I lost myself in sweet dreams, not nightmares. The pain would ease and I could sleep and drift off to never-never land. I loved that morphine. It was like I couldn't live without it all the days in the hospital. Every time I was awake I wanted my *fix*. But after a few days the doctor took me off morphine. The other pain killers I took with a glass of water didn't work as well as morphine. Not having it made me cry and I became depressed being so alone in a bed not my own. I couldn't move, immobilized with my seriously damaged leg hanging in the air. If I had to move out of bed, I had to get nurse's aides to lower my leg, and then painfully slide myself onto a wheel or bed-pan chair, only if the aides could help me do so. I was a *prisoner* in that bed in agony, both physically and mentally. The thing that helped keep me sane and retreat from pain was morphine, it kept me from tears.

I had visitors, my mother, sister, and Aunt Queen. Trina Dobbs, Pumpkin, came alone to see and cheer me up, they came to visit me when they had bus fare for the long ride. When Pumpkin came she would talk non-stop about anything and everything. I didn't want her to go when visiting time was over. Her sugary-toned voice once annoyed me. Now it was a respite from me feeling alone. She made me laugh even when I was in pain. I wished that her soft and sweet smelling body was lying beside me to keep me company. Pumpkin always left me with a warm kiss to my lips. I always felt liked me for who I was as a friend, whether I played basketball or not. But playing it was so much a part of my identity and I felt that *identity* slipping away.

My mother and Aunt Queen in chairs on opposite sides of my bed, they usually came together after Auntie got off from work. They both had worried looks on their faces, which made me worry. My father never came to visit me. My mother always said he was working. I knew she was making an excuse for him. I never forgave him for that.

Coach brought a carload of teammates to see me once, which was enough for me. I didn't want to see them. It was difficult that I couldn't be with them on a basketball court again. Seeing them made me more depressed I think Coach Vic had sensed this, and he never brought the team to see me again.

———————

"You got a busted knee. So you think you got it bad? It could be worse. Get ready to move your life on without these games you love to play. There are people out here worse off than you," It was Aunt Queen's *pep talk* on one of her visits with me. It was one of the times I wanted to tell my favorite Auntie, to *shut the hell up*. But I knew she was trying to help me feel better about my situation, but her words were ones I didn't want to hear. And Auntie should have known the *games* were important for me, not for her. I wasn't ready to move on without basketball in my life no matter what anyone said.

"And stop worrying about Smokey," she added to the *pep talk*. "He's with God. I thought, *Huh, I bet Smokey would be surprised to see someone he didn't believe in* "The dead don't need the living worrying about them. Grow up." Her words hurt my feelings. Aunt Queen used her words, not her hands to help me move on. Mama would have slapped some sense into me, if she had been at my bedside.

Coach Vic dropped in alone one of the last days I was in the hospital. He brought with him homework and books that I needed for the time I missed from school. Doing school work was the last thing on my mind.

"How are you doing Bevenue?" Coach never called me Mercer.

"I'm doin' okay Coach." But I really wasn't *okay*. I was miserable, depressed, and scared. The only exercise I got was getting in a bed pan chair to relieve myself while they changed my bed linen. I couldn't walk with the heavy cast on my leg without using crutches. It was so difficult and painful to move. I subconsciously wondered if I'd ever walk again, let alone run down a basketball court.

"Hell Bevenue, you look like you're feeling sorry for yourself. I talked to your surgeon while he was making rounds in the hospital before I came to see you. He wasn't going to talk to me about your condition because I wasn't family. All he would tell me was that the surgery went well and you are going to have a long recovery. I really didn't know what that meant. I wanted him to tell me something about when you'd be able to get back on the court.

"Coach, he told me that I'd probably never play basketball again because of the injury I sustained. The doctor said that I'd have a limp when I walked with some difficulty, let alone run." I choked back the tears that welled up in my eyes. I didn't want to embarrass myself in front of man that probably never cried in his life.

"Did you believe what the doctor said?"

"I don't know, I just feel like he's right, 'cause the pain is so bad, My whole body hurts every time I move. In my mind I see myself still playing the game, but my body says no."

"Keep this between me and you Bevenue. I almost died the first time I was injured in the war, but of course I didn't. I recovered from the bullet wounds and eager to go back into battle. I was shot again and stabbed with a rifle saber a few times in combat. The doctors said I'd lost a lot of blood the second time around in the hospital. All I wanted to do was fight again despite their feelings about my health. I had a wife and son back here in Eau Claire. So, I decided not to push my luck. The Marines shipped me home. The purpose of me telling you this Bevenue is that I never gave up fighting after almost dying twice. So, what do think I'm trying to tell you?

Never go to war? Is what my answer would have be if Coach had a sense of humor. But he was not the kind of man to joke with. He probably would have made me run laps in the hospital halls if I'd said what I was thinking. I was serious about not going to war. Some boys I knew went to Vietnam, and those that came back to the city were physically and mentally out of sorts, like they couldn't believe they were back at home.

"Yeah Coach, mind over matter was more important despite what anyone says." Those were also my Aunt Queen's words after Smokey died, when my heart ached so badly.

"Very good Bevenue," he said like he couldn't believe I would answer that way. There are some college coaches looking at recruiting some guys on the team, but now I think they are backing off from you because of your knee injury." It was not what I wanted to hear, because it only made me feel worse. Coach was always straight with me. He didn't like playing around with sympathetic words only the reality of my situation.

"Bevenue, you have two years to prove to yourself that you deserve to play college basketball. You need to tell yourself that you can do this mainly by yourself. All I can promise you is that once you make it back to my gym, I will work your ass off. Bevenue, it is going to be hard. But I do have an incentive for you, if you show me you have heart, I promise I'll get you into college.

He was the only man that made a promise to me that he kept. Coach barely got me into Rutgers College in New Jersey. I however, earned a partial basketball scholarship and an academic grant to go to the school. Coach's ex-Marine friend was the head basketball coach there. When I talked to him he said I'd probably be a bench warmer on the team. And asked me if I *still wanted to come?* It was like he was doing me a favor by letting me come to his school. I knew nothing about the Rutgers or exactly where it was. The Rutgers coach had no idea what was inside of me. But I was going to prove that I could play ball. I was going to college out of state and that's all that mattered.

Chapter 27

The block I grew up on was still a dreary and messy place in the summer after junior year of college. Some of the wood frame houses had been painted since then. They did brighten the block a bit, but the paint couldn't hide how ugliness of the dwellings. Kids still played on dirt lawns and in the streets like I did with Smokey when we were young. He was in my thoughts every day since his death about seven years ago. Smokey's house across the street from mine seemed smaller and haunting. Still, I was glad to be home.

Hog Hoffmann's Butcher Shop and Ziegler's Grocery were now owned by black people. I was glad that to hear that Hog Hoffmann was gone from the block. Smokey hated the old German for sleeping with his mother when she couldn't pay the rent on the house he owned. And I disliked Ziegler because he treated me like a *colored boy* when I used to go into his store.

I sat with my mother on our porch and asked her about Mr. Hoffmann and Mr. Ziegler. She said she kind of missed them because she couldn't run a tab at the stores anymore.

"Them goddamned Negroes are worse than them crackers trying to beat money out of poor folks. But since you been off to college the past couple of years, we don't need that much goddamn food." Mama said laughing out loud. It was great to hear her laugh and see her smile. She looked happier than I'd ever seen her. I wasn't a boy anymore, but a man capable of taking care of myself. Mama didn't need to worry about me so much. It was only the second time I'd been back in two years.

"Mercer, you look so handsome and smart, me and your Daddy is proud of you." I felt embarrassed and surprised by her words. There had not been much compassion in my house growing up. *Now is better than never*, I conceded.

It felt great to be here. I was more appreciative of the place now, after living in the congestion of people on the East Coast. Some people say "you can never come home again and expect things to be the same as you left it." They were right. Home seemed better now; the air was fresher, the people friendlier, and the sky cleaner than back East. I had it a lot better growing up poor here than in comparison to where my college roommate and teammate Wyatt Wilmore grew up in New York City.

Wyatt and I liked each other a lot. He was intelligent and straightforward with me and confident while being humble. He was a freshman just like me. Wyatt was more sophisticated than I was about life. He once said to me that "living in New York I had to grow up fast." He was more man than boy.

Wyatt's skin was the color of a West Indian eggplant. He stood about six-foot-seven. He would have been an imposing figure here in Milwaukee. I saw and played basketball against guys Wyatt's height and more in pick-up games on campus. So, his height was not uncommon out here. I stood six-foot-three and I felt short standing next to him. Wyatt's body was sinewy, with muscles that made him look like a sculpture of black onyx. He used that hard body to push around guys on the court when he went for rebounds. Yet, Wyatt moved with finesse when the basketball was in his hands when he was offense. He was the best baller I'd ever played with.

Wyatt never lifted weights and ate what he wanted. He never seemed to gain weight. I, on the other hand, had to run laps around the gym just to keep the pounds off. And I had become addicted to bagels and cream cheeses.

Wyatt had perfect looking perfect looking white teeth that shown every time he smiled, which was often. I was envious. My teeth were so bad that I had to cover my mouth when I laughed. Wyatt was just an optimistic person, nothing seemed to bother him. It was like he never seemed to be depressed. I asked Wyatt, "Why he was always happy all the time? I never see you upset except on the court." In his deep tone with that New Yorker accent, he said, "Mercer, I don't dwell on shit I can't control, but when I'm playing ball I am in charge of what I do on the hardwood." I worried about everything all the time when I first came to Rutgers, and for the most part, I didn't hide my feelings. But before my freshman year at Rutgers was over

I began to emulate his attitude about taking things as they come. If it wasn't for Wyatt, I wouldn't have made it through those first three years at school. In a way, without Smokey as a friend growing up I wouldn't have the determination to go to college. The tragedy of his death helped me appreciate being alive.

"Hey man, I didn't know there were any black people in Wisconsin." I kind of laughed about that statement at first, but I think Wyatt was serious.

On a Friday afternoon after we came back to our dorm room after study hall. We sat on the foot of our bunk beds because it would be uncomfortable facing each other because his legs were so long. I told Wyatt about my raggedy neighborhood. He didn't cringe when I described my house with the holes in the walls or bathroom floor in the bathroom that I could see through to the basement. I told him about the bad plumbing that ran dirty water when it was cold outside. And I said there were cockroaches and mice that had the run of our rundown house.

He didn't react to anything I said until I told him that "my best friend Smokey drowned in the Milwaukee River. And how I thought it wasn't an accident." Wyatt just raised his eyebrows a little. But when I mentioned that I had a *Red Flyer* wagon that I called the welfare wagon he grinned at the name I'd given it.

"What the hell does a wagon have to do with welfare?" He asked me.

"Man, I used it to go to the welfare food warehouse with my mother on Saturday mornings once or twice a month to get food. We used to get powdered eggs and milk, dried pinto beans and northern beans; oatmeal and cereal in big brown boxes; cartons of commodity cheese, and tins of spam." Wyatt said, "I'm getting hungry as hell listening to that food talk." I burst out laughing. I'm thinking, *a man after my own heart* as he chuckled along with me. It was hard to make my welfare wagon story serious again after that. My tone had become less important as I tried to continue anyway as Wyatt smiled at me while rubbing his stomach. In spite of him mocking my wagon story, I kept telling it. "I dragged that heavy-ass stuff all over the damn neighborhood. And sometimes we went out of the way to pick stuff up at a farmers market many blocks away from my house. I told him that my mother would nag me all the time I was pulling that wagon. Do you know the worst part of those Saturday mornings? It was people seeing me with that wagon load of welfare food. My mother acted like it was okay to be on welfare." I wanted Wyatt to feel my pain. He took an exaggerated yawn and looked at me like he was going burst out laughing at any moment.

Wyatt looked amused after hearing my *hard life* story. "Mercer, you're just a little-city boy." He said jokingly with a smirk on his face. He reminded me of Smokey with that wry grin. I was embarrassed and a little offended by what he said. I just sat on my end of the bed without saying another word like a sullen child. I was soon to learn that my upbringing was so trivial in comparison to what I saw how some people lived in New York City.

"Mercer, I am going to take you on a field trip to the *big city*. You haven't been off campus yet, have you? This campus is not the real world." He said.

"Nah man, I haven't been anywhere."

"We're going to New York City after lunch, if you aren't scared. You'll need some money for the buses and subways, maybe fifteen or twenty dollars. But you need to dress like you don't have money. And I don't want your little-city ass looking up at the tall buildings like a tourist. Man, people will come up to you and try and sell you all kinds of shit, from watches to reefer, if you look out of place. There are people in the streets that make their living begging for change. So keep your money in two pockets, but keep your tokens and bus fare money in your socks, because if someone picks your pocket, you'll be begging for coins to get back to campus. It can be a long-assed walk. I know we're some big boys, but some of those *crazies* don't care how big we are if they're desperate. So, you still want to go to the *big-city*?" Wyatt laughed loudly.

I said, "Bullshit Wyatt, New York City can't be that much different than Milwaukee." At least that's what I told myself. "Yeah man, I'm not afraid to go." I was curious to find out what could be different between and small city than a big one. Maybe I was a little apprehensive.

The buses and subways Wyatt and I took to NYC were jammed with people of all skin colors, and there were odors I smelled that made my head spin, and made me want to faint. However, there was no room to fall down. People were so close that someone could pick my pocket. Wyatt seemed to enjoy the rides on the trip. He was in his element of chaos, sights, and fragrances. I watched him closely; I didn't want him getting off at a stop without me. Wyatt said, *he'd take care of me.* I trusted his words.

I saw graffiti on houses, walls, and on the sides of subway trains except in movies. Some of the drawings and scribbling were colorful, like works of art. And some of the writings on these things that were both profound and profane. I had never seen much graffiti back in Milwaukee except for few gang signs on garages in the neighborhood. In NYC subway stations to me had the best graffiti, artworks that could be hung in museums. Wyatt, like the other people around seemed not to appreciate what I saw as they passed by. I was drawn to the paintings I saw on things that made those things more colorful and beautiful. I never got to the point where I ignored the graffiti when I walked by the creations. I was envious that I didn't have the skills to draw like those street artists,

There were people that lived down in the subways, Wyatt said, "that's why it smells like piss and vomit." The foul smells didn't bother Wyatt. The odors bothered me, but not enough to make me say anything. Wyatt did say, "Mercer, you better act like you belong.

If you don't it could mean trouble. In these streets, people lookin' for new meat to take advantage of."

We went above ground from the subway to an ocean of humanity moving everywhere and nowhere on the streets. People of different hues looked over their shoulders at some real or imagined threats as they hurriedly moved in a constantly crammed motion, like their movements were synchronized. Without missing a beat they deftly stepped over unfortunate people lying on sidewalks like they were bags of garbage. Wyatt made sure I kept in step with the frenetic masses.

I told Wyatt "I didn't think I could step over somebody lying in the streets without stopping to help."

"Mercer, when you are in this city, you have to keep moving no matter what is in your way. We learned to mind our own business and worry only about what is front of us."

I kept moving alongside and over obstacles in my way, human and not. But I was still unable to ignore the *new world* I was walking in. I could not help from noticing the mass of humanity I was trying to maneuver through on the streets. It was difficult to keep pace with the thick, rapid flow of people, while trying to keep up with Wyatt; who faced forward as he rapidly moved upstream like a spawning salmon.

There were so people speaking different languages and some of the clothing they wore looked foreign, I didn't feel like I wasn't in New York City but in some other country. The skin colors of the people were all spectrums of the rainbow. They reminded me of the minnows I saw in the Milwaukee River back home near the shore where Smokey and I used to dip our feet in the water.

I saw men embrace and kiss each other in Greenwich Village. And there were women holding hands and kissing as they walked down the streets, like they were love birds. I was definitely not back in Milwaukee. I was shocked to see such a public expression of affection by people of the same gender. And those people didn't seem to give a damn what others thought.

Wyatt and I bought a slice of pizza and a soft drink from a food cart in front of a pizzeria in the Village before we got on a bus to Queens. He was surprised to know that they didn't have food carts back in Milwaukee or that pizza wasn't sold by the slice. On the bus I noticed the buildings of the city for the first time. The buildings hovered in the clouds, and I finally saw the true vision of the Empire State Building, and other skyscrapers that were some of the tallest buildings in the world. Wyatt had me so trained to focus on what was happening around me that I failed to look up, but couldn't help but do so. *Only tourists look up,* Wyatt's words rung in my head. I couldn't help it. Everything was so interesting to this *small city boy.*

We then got off a bus a few blocks away from where Wyatt grew up. "Man, I lived on the twentieth floor in the housing projects, with my parents and two younger sisters. Sometimes the elevator didn't work. And gangs would charge kids for using the stairs. My sisters had to wait for me until after basketball or football practice, because their school was near mine. We'd come home together. If my father wasn't working, he would meet us at the front of our building. My Daddy is a big man that nobody messes with him in the projects. You just don't go to my building unannounced, especially with a new face like yours. So, you better be with somebody that lives there if you came around," Wyatt also added, "With all these goddamn people piled on top of one another in small apartments of thirty floors of folks in this project building. There is bound to be cockroaches and other nasty shit crawling around, and we don't need more *pests* around like strange people to make our lives more miserable." I thought. *How could people live like this?*

We were strolling through a park where people were moving in every direction when I saw this guy to seem to float on air instead without his feet hitting the ground walking nearby. "Wyatt, who is that guy waving at?"

"Yeah, I saw him." Wyatt waved back. I did too out of reflex like I knew him too. I did this all the time, waving at people back home to be polite.

Wyatt said, "Well, he knows me, and probably thinks he knows you too. We played basketball together growing up on the playgrounds. He was the greatest basketball player you'll never see play in college or the pros. His name is Earl Manigault, but people call him "The Goat," He was the best basketball player I've ever seen, even better than the most of the professional players that came to play on the asphalt. But drugs and drinking messed up his talent, using that shit. A lot of my friends that I grew up with are hooked on drugs or dealing that crap. The Goat never looked like he could do the things he could do on the court being slight of build and standing about six one, but he was up to all the challenges of the so-called big boys. He had springs for legs, he'd probably take a bet that he could touch the moon if the money was right," Wyatt laughed loudly.

"Some of the girls that were classmates of mine in elementary and high school have sold their bodies just to feed themselves and children or get another fix. You told me about your best friend that died? Well I've had a lot of *best friends*, and some are in colleges, and some in colleges. And many of my friends are lost to the streets, dead, or in prison. I've lost count," Wyatt said. It was the first time I'd seen sadness in his face.

We walked without speaking while I took in the surroundings for awhile until we reached the business district of Queens. There was garbage piled high on the edge of sidewalks and overflowing garbage cans. The trash climbed the walls in alleys like some putrid smelly vines. There were dumpsters in the alleys on the side of bakeries, pizza joints and bagel shops. The smells were good and bad at the same time. The odors made me hungry on some level, but made me gag on another. Wyatt looked like he was in heaven, basking in the glow of the surroundings.

"Mercer, can you imagine my big ass looking in garbage cans and dumpsters for discarded food? Man, after my father lost his factory job in Long Island, I had to rummage through some of these dumpsters and compete with the rats the size of puppies and cockroaches as big as mice for discarded food. I wasn't the only person looking for day old bagels and bakery, and half-eaten pizzas. I tried to find anything eatable to feed us until my father could find work. Shit, my family might went hungry many a day but we didn't starve. Besides, man or rodent that went through the garbage would mess with me because I was so big." Wyatt said laughing at himself."

I could tell Wyatt was proud of his food gathering skills because his chest stuck out like a black rooster. I realized carrying welfare food in my *Red Flyer* wagon didn't compare what he had gone through growing up in Queens. I couldn't have imagined going through garbage for food. After hearing Wyatt's story, I wasn't ashamed or embarrassed about my youthful plight anymore. He never mentioned that story to me even in jest ever again. It was like he trusted me to understand his perspective of where he was coming from. I never repeated his story to anyone. Nor did we talk again about the *welfare wagon* or Smokey again. I would never take for granted growing up a *little-city boy versus a big- city boy any day.*

Chapter 28

I once despised Milwaukee but, not so much since I'd been away. I saw cities on the East Coast that made my broken down neighborhood look like a resort area. And I'd never thought that I would be homesick. I missed family and some of my friends, especially Trina "Pumpkin" Dobbs. She was the only friend to who took time to write me while I was at college. Pumpkin had earned a scholarship to Howard University after graduating from one of the best public school in Milwaukee. I think she wanted to be a doctor or a lawyer or own her own business. Pumpkin had plans for her future. Pumpkin probably could be a great lawyer, she loved to talk and argue. She always took a stance on any topic when we were growing up.

Being back home also brought back memories of Smokey. Fortunately, playing basketball, work-study, meeting new people, and going back and forth to New York City on my own didn't leave me much time to think about Smokey. I was happy about that. Now that I was back on the block, old memories came to roost in my mind. The pang in my heart was no longer as profound as it once was as I looked over at his ramshackle house from my porch, a new coat of white paint but still the same.

I went off to college thinking that the grass had to be greener on the other side. I was wrong; there was very little grass anywhere outside of the Rutgers campus. Concrete and asphalt dominated the landscape off most of the cities out East. Some of the houses that I saw people live in were far worse than the one I grew up in, my house was a mansion comparison.

I always thought the streets where I grew up as messy with things scattered everywhere on dirt lawns and in alleys that should have been in garbage cans. It didn't compare to what I saw in NYC where debris, like old furniture and appliances on sidewalks in some of the places in the city. It wasn't just to enough to side step that junk; trying to dodge homeless people wrapped in filthy clothes or blankets on sidewalks was disheartening.

I was happy be back amongst people that spoke English in most places. In this city faces were familiar. Yet, New York City was cosmopolitan with people from all over the world; so many ethnic groups and cultures to count in a lifetime. And I loved it.

I missed sitting on my front porch watching my little world go by, which looked even smaller now that I'd grown in more ways than one. I could glance across at Smokey's house now without crying. I knew he would never stride across the street to talk *shit* with me on my front porch about basketball or Phoebe Westbrook or Pumpkin. God I still missed him, just not so much anymore though Smokey probably would say "that God wasn't real." However, I could sit here and reminisce about the days Smokey used to sit next to me in a chair on my front porch.

I was looking forward to eating my mother's cooking at our kitchen table, which was a newer version of the old one we had growing up. There was a new stove and vinyl flooring in the kitchen. And the tiny bathroom was still that, but the walls were a bright beige color and the wood flooring was linoleum which was a light shade of brown with no opening gash around the toilet to see to the basement. The toilet and bathroom sink were new and a sparkling white.

My sister Birdie and even my father would talk and joke, and make noise that families do around the kitchen table over food, something my father never did when I was in the house. He asked me *how I was doing in college and if I was playing much on the basketball team? It took me being gone for him to care what I was up to.* I was glad to hear that he seemed to have changed from an indifferent man into a father by the way he interacted with Birdie. He may have even missed me once I went off to college. I felt better about him and understood why he was stern with me as a boy. Maybe he was a shrewd man that I never gave him credit for growing up because Daddy made me a person that would only depend on me for the choices I made in life.

———————————

Phoebe Westbrook, the girl I once adored, had recently moved back into her old house down the street after being gone for about seven years according to my mother. She left her baby, that most assumed was Smokey's, down in Nashville with her mother's childless sister. Mama had said that Phoebe finished high school down there,

Now that Smokey was dead, she didn't have to tell anyone who the father of her baby was, I guess I wouldn't want to tell anyone "that my step-father raped me." I hadn't seen her since the day after junior high graduation when we talked about Smokey, friendship, and her story about her step-father's sexual abuse on my front porch. I promised Phoebe I would never tell anyone the sad truth about her situation, even though I wasn't happy with her at the time. *Time heals old wounds* as people often said, but I never forgave her for letting people think that Smokey was the father of her child. I don't think that *wound* will never *heal* within me.

I had asked Mama about Phoebe, "She'd been back from Nashville, maybe about a year or so. Her mama said the baby boy stayed down there with her sister. Phoebe, her mama and sister, moved back into their house down the street after their step-daddy left town. Phoebe's mama had the house in her name when her first husband died before you were born, she let her husband stay in the house until they were ready to come back home. Nobody knows where he went and I don't think anyone cares."

"I thought I'd never see her again. I haven't thought much about Phoebe since I've been gone" I said to Mama.

"Mercer, Phoebe has changed after all she's been through." *Hell Mama, I've been through a lot of crap too. I know it changed me, hopefully for the better,* is what I wanted to say. And I felt bad that I was only thinking about my own feelings. Phoebe had gone through far worse experiences I had. And I suspect her experiences were far more destructive to her spirit than mine.

I walked down the block to Phoebe's house, wondering when there would be a friendly encounter between us. It was a Friday evening and I wanted to take her to a movie or out to get some food somewhere. When I reached the bottom of her porch stairs, she was coming out the screen door. She was dressed like a church matron in a white blouse that covered her neck and a long black skirt that hung below her knees. Phoebe wore black comfortable looking shoes like the ones I'd seen the women ushers wear in church, and had a bible was sticking out of her big black purse. I guess Mama was right when she said *Phoebe had changed.*

I think I startled her when she turned around and saw me standing there as if I were a stranger in the dark ready to do her harm. It was a cold feeling that I got from her.

"Mercer?" she said sounding like she was surprised to see me.

She had the same sultry eyes, and perfect light-brown skin that I remembered. Phoebe's lips looked luscious and unadorned with lipstick. Her beautiful auburn hair was in a bun and but no longer hanged below her shoulders.

"Yeah Phoebe, it's me. You look fine as hell."

She came down the stairs to meet me where I stood looking at her. I reached out my arms to accept a friendly hug, but she brushed through my arms like I wasn't even there.

"Is something wrong Phoebe?" I thought that maybe I was musty, but I sniffed myself and smelled nothing but deodorant and a little *Old Spice* cologne. *Damn, I'd give myself a hug.* "No, Mercer, you startled me, I am really glad to see you. I think about you and Smokey always being together growing up. After seeing you standing there, I *saw* Smokey too.

I just wanted to put my arms around Phoebe, but she wasn't receptive to my touch. So, I tried to drum up of conversation with her. "Hey girl, you look like you going to church on a Wednesday night," I always had keen observations. It was a stupid thing to say. And I wished I had asked Phoebe anything at all.

"Yes Mercer, I am going to church, the Pentecostal church on the corner. Gaddis' father in now the minister in the church and Gaddis is a deacon. He wants to be a preacher like his father."

Just the mention of Gaddis' name took me aback: it brought me back to the day Smokey drowned in Estabrook Park. Licorice Fletcher, also a former friend of mine was with them on that tragic day. I never forgave them not watching my friend before he had his so-called *accident* in the Milwaukee River. I felt the red-hot anger swell inside me like a raging fire, but I refused to let her know what I was thinking about Gaddis the *church boy. How could Phoebe join the church that she made fun of when we were growing up?* And I wondered if she thought Gaddis, who she also made *fun of,* because of his crude manners, selfish ways, and filthy words, especially for a church boy when we were kids was now a different kind of man?

"Mercer, what are you thinking?"

I must have blanked out for a moment and said, "Just remembering things."

"Well, Mercer, I have to rush off to church, I'm running late for choir practice and usher board meeting. I'll stop by your house when I can."

"Maybe we can go see a film or have lunch one day, I'm home for the summer."

"Mercer, I don't go to the movies anymore. And I don't go out to eat with boys that are not in from my church." Then she turned her back on me a walked passed my house to the Pentecostal church on the corner.

———————

My cousin Booker Dunbar, who had been discharged from the Army after being in the service for two years in Vietnam, Booker came by to see me when he found out I was back for the summer. He wasn't the kind of guy that came by to visit; I would usually go into the house if I saw him coming down the street when I was growing up. But he seemed different now that he was sitting next to me on the front porch. Booker's voice was soft, not abrasive as it once had been as the bully I knew. There was no edge in his mannerisms, he seemed meek. We made small talk about me being in college, friends and family, but nothing about Vietnam. A fast moving car backfired like a shotgun had gone off as it passed in the street in front of us as it passed by in the street. Booker jumped out of the chair and crouched as he ran into doorway of my house. He disappeared so fast even before I had a chance to react to the loud noise. Moments later, after the car was well out of sight and sound, Booker was peering out the screen door. He appeared fragile. It scared me to see him like that, instead of the stupid and fearless bully I had grown up to dislike, but he wasn't those things anymore that I could see.

Chapter 29

Salty sweat stung my eyes and drenched my tee shirt completely. My lungs heaved as I sucked in hot air that somehow, now had weight. I breathed in the subtle odor of tar, not as strong as I ever remembered. The steaming asphalt was smooth and dark with no divots or cracks. I nestled myself in the cranny of the wide, tall spruce tree with my back against its bark, and spread my legs over the thick above ground roots. It was uncomfortable, but I was wider and taller since I last sat in the stomach of that tree.

Franklin Square playground, the *Square*, did not have the same sensation of being here as it once did. The aesthetics of a playground that attracted boys had changed for me. The ugliness of the *Square* was not there anymore. It was hard to explain, it just seemed so easy to play here not like it was when I was boy.

The tree I was under was the last one standing. It was the only place to find shade on this asphalt desert. Smokey and I, along with other boys, used to play basketball here from dawn to dusk; it was our home away from home growing up. Sadly, the Square looked desolate now.

There were new looking half-moon white backboards each with one hooked black metal post that suspended the basketball hoops ten feet above the asphalt. When Smokey and I played here as a boy, there were old wooden square dull gray backboards, bracketed on each side by thin silver-gray metal posts holding them up. Many a boy had lost teeth or been knocked silly by one of those post, me included. I remember the dark round smudges that we would make on the backboards with a basketball when we shot hoops in the rain. Now it was evident the playground was not a basketball battleground anymore; no character, no dirt, no dust, and no attitude. It seemed too sterile, just like the playgrounds in the suburbs.

There was no hint of the history that tough and rough poor black boys ever played serious games of war on these courts like when I was a boy. If the wood pole lights stayed on over the courts, sometime when they weren't, we would play deep into the night by moonlight. All we needed was a basketball.

Often in the daytime the sun was unforgiving on the Square and there was very little breeze. Yet, the weather never deterred us from playing basketball on the courts as kids. On this afternoon the only sound of life was my heavy breathing. This used to be a bustling playground but not on this day. In the winter kids would shovel snow off a court and shoot baskets in their winter clothing. I guess I'm skeptical, because I just don't envision black kids playing ball on these courts on winter days.

I guess black boys these days had other things to do on a Sunday afternoon. I used to go to Sunday school at St. Matthews Methodist church in the morning, and would head home to change out of my *church clothes* and to pick-up Smokey so we could go to the playground together.

When Smokey and I were young the playground was our church. It was our haven from all the disappointments of living in poverty. And foolish boys like us hoped that basketball was going to alleviate the pressure and give us the chance of getting out of the city. It worked for me, but for other black boys not so much. Still the *Square* provided an escape from our sometimes dysfunctional lives. My family, friends, and teachers let me know that they thought basketball wasn't going to get me anywhere in life. I was lucky.

———————

Now my right knee looked like a brown lumpy softball with a crooked stitched-up line running down it. It hurt every day. The gnarled knee, the bumps, the jagged scar, and rough blemishes on it reminded me how imperfect I was, just like the rest of humanity. I was on the playground to work out before the basketball season; I sprinted, up and down the hot asphalt of the court, jumping as many times as I could to touch the hoop with my fingertips; and I took jump shots until my arms and legs hurt. Unfortunately, no work out was going to make me faster or jump higher. I was putting in the effort to keep up the illusion that I could play at a high level for the final basketball season at Rutgers.

I thought about my high school basketball coach as I sat in that tree. He made a deal with me at my hospital bedside as I recovered after knee surgery in my sophomore year of high school. He said that "if I worked hard in the classroom, foremost, and on the hardwood floors of the basketball courts, secondly, he would get me into college." At that time I was worried about walking again. Coach had said "mind over matter" was his motto. Coach kept his word. And without helping me believe in myself, I don't think I would be in college.

I wiped the sweat on my face and arms which was salty white and sticky. I reached for my wet blue wash cloth which I had soaked with bubbler water when I entered the playground. I took it from under the seat pouch of my new black ten-speed bike. The cloth felt good as I wiped the wet places on my body. I felt clean again.

My bike had a nice silver colored carrier rack that could clamp down on my basketball. A far cry from the bike I use to have, the one I let Smokey borrow on the day he died at Estabrook Park. I saved my college work-study money to buy this bike. I was reminded me how I saved my snow shoveling money as a boy to buy my first bike and how Smokey spent his money to buy a shark-skinned colored suit. He sure liked to be flashy.

There was a pair of sunglasses I bought back in Queens that I also took out of the pouch. Now the dark shades hid my eyes which made me feel like I was an unidentified person, which I liked. There was also a nice and dry two inch joint wrapped in a small piece of aluminum foil and a box of stick matches in that same pouch. The marijuana was a gift from Wyatt, my college roommate and basketball teammate at Rutgers. He was the best player I'd ever played with, including Sweets Ingram from back in high school. There were professional basketball teams looking to draft him into the pros. I was happy, and maybe a little envious of him. My love for the game was still inside me, it was just too painful for me to play well consistently anymore. I felt my best days on the playing this game was behind me. I got what I needed from playing basketball and it was well-worth the agony to get into college.

Back at college Wyatt loved to smoke marijuana, I didn't. But on occasion I did light up a joint. Smoking weed in public was no big deal out East, especially around college campuses. There was too much turmoil going on at schools like protests of the Vietnam War and the Civil Rights Movement, for the police to bother with college kids smoking weed.

Now that I was back In Milwaukee where black people could get arrested just for being in a place where white cops didn't want you to be. I wasn't afraid of getting arrested for smoking a joint here on the Square now. Now cops rarely showed up even for emergencies in this part of the community, and from I knew being back in the city, nothing had changed. So, as I sat in the nook up the tree I felt safe to fire up.

I lit up my *gift*. I felt untouchable inside the tree. Sucking in that stinky smoke into my lungs swirled around me. I felt mellow after a few deep puffs, because it was really strong. My mind floated somewhere into a daydream, imagining that the world looked better than it was. There was more than sweat running down my cheeks. I didn't feel maudlin but tears had welled up in my eyes. It wasn't that I was sad, in fact I felt a little mellow. I guess it was because I knew my basketball journey was coming to an end and I felt relieved. I forgot about my ailing knees as the sweat and tears ran down my cheeks. And I was imagining that I was cat lying in sun-soaked window sill. *I was in a tree trunk not in a window. I couldn't be tripping after only a few puffs.* Maybe I thought was tired and the heat of the day were only having an effect on me.

A vaguely familiar voice snuck up on me somewhere behind the tree. I'm thinking, am I really hearing somebody or are these words in my head? Whatever was happening, there was no way I was going to stub-out this joint, but it had gone out anyway. I shouldn't have smoked this stuff in the open. I shouldn't have taken this kind of risk in this city.

"Say brothah, let me have a hit off that sweet smelling bud," said the voice now in front of me looking at smoke rather than my face.

Damn, I ain't going crazy.

His dark skin was rough looking and he looked "sickly" as my mother used to say. He had lips that were crusty and cracked, like they hadn't felt water in awhile. *I'll be damned if I let this crusty-lipped Negro put those lips on this reefer.*

Licorice Fletcher was skinnier than I remembered after not talking to him almost seven years ago, the day of Smokey's death. He was the thinnest kid I ever knew growing up. It didn't seem possible that he was now skinnier. He could've floated away if there were a strong wind blowing across the playground. The blue cotton long sleeved shirt and the khaki slacks he wore were dirty and smelled like hot garbage that I smelled in the hot breeze. It was definitely a smell that would have made me gag if I wasn't so buzzed. He needed to stand somewhere else, preferably outside the Square.

"Come on man; let me get a drag. I just want a little taste of….. He stopped talking and looked at me closely, liked he'd seen a ghost wearing sunglasses. "Mercer, Mercer Bevenue?"

"Yeah Licorice, it's me."

He looked weak and strung out. Yet, I found it hard for me to care. There was no sympathy in my feelings towards him. I thought I was better than that. Licorice looked like a pitiful a cockroach to me. And as much as I wanted to deny him a smoke, I offered him the rest of my joint, but he didn't take it. I wanted him to move on. He just stood in front of like he had forgotten what he asked for.

"Man, I am so happy to see you, I been hearin' around that you playing good ball in college. I saw the box scores from some of your basketball games in the newspaper. Man, you can still score some points. Mercer, you did good to get your ass outta' Milwaukee."

"Yeah Licorice, after Smokey died I wanted get away from this place for a while," I said to letting Licorice know that I had not forgotten Smokey's death.

"Mercer, I know you blame me and Gaddis for Smokey's drowning," Licorice said. I barely listened to his words as I looked over the *Square* knowing that it would be the last time I would come here. It had come to this time I had to rid myself of the past in more ways than one. But there was one question that hung in mind, *was it an accident that Smokey drowned like Gaddis and Licorice said?*

"I should have done more to stop Gaddis. I should have tackled his fat ass before he pushed Smokey into the water," said a regretful sounding Licorice."

"What…what do you mean you "should have done more to stop Gaddis? Why you want to tell me this shit after all this time." I said with an edge to my voice.

"Mercer, 'cause I was scared to say anything to anyone back then. Now, I don't give a shit if everyone knows what happened. It ain't goin' to bring back Smokey. What people gonna do, put me in jail for not telling the truth about a black boy? Just look at me Mercer.

My life is fucked up. Gaddis said it was an accident that Smokey drowned in the river. I just agreed with him knowing it was wrong. There were always consequences for the lies we couldn't get away with. Our parents or grandparents or teachers or other adults that weren't white would use corporal punishment to discipline us even for the smallest untruth.

I agreed with Licorice, black boys survival depended on lies to everyone, even God. And Lord knows Gaddis, the *church boy,* lied to God every time he went to church which was a lot. He blamed others when he got into trouble, especially his friends for a series of childhood misdeeds he often initiated. Gaddis never seemed to regret or admit his guilt, even when caught red-handed. His father would beat him for lying to him, and yet it didn't stop him from doing it. My mother beat me too when I messed up, but she never made me go to church to ask God for forgiveness, like Gaddis's father made him do. God knew that I fucked-up and that Mama punished me for it. I didn't stop lying after getting whooped, and neither did Gaddis.

"After Smokey drowned Gaddis's family shipped his chunky ass down South to live with relatives, probably 'cause they knew he had lied about what had happened. If he stayed, I'd…I'd might have tried to kill him for what he did to Smokey, and me." Licorice sounded serious. I doubted that Licorice had to courage to murder someone. I knew enough about him that it was only hate that he was speaking of.

Licorice continued talking about what happened like he wanted to get the past all out of his conscious; "Who was it that I was supposed to talk too about what happened, the cops? I sure wasn't goin' to tell his parents. They thought Gaddis walked on water. You know what they did? Gaddis's daddy gave my parents two-hundred dollars to keep me from saying anything about what really went on at Estabrook. I didn't get a goddamn dime of that money."

The police, what was I goin' to tell them? Was that me and Gaddis snuck up behind Smokey to scare him while his back was turned? Shit man, the cops don't give a shit about black boys, we was just a bunch of niggers to them. They wasn't goin' to go out of their way to investigate how a black boy died. Gaddis pushed him off that rock in the rapids, not me. The water flushed him under like he was a terd in a toilet bowl. I didn't touch Smokey and I couldn't save him as I watched his head bob up and down in the river. That sight will haunt me forever." We made sounds like we were barking dogs, and you know how Smokey hated dogs. The barking scared Smokey and he turned around on the big slippery rock as Gaddis kind of pushed him in the water, I think he only wanted to get Smokey wet but the rapids took him under. We was only playing."

"Gaddis was a church boy and I was just a raggedy-ass boy that never set foot in a church. And Gaddis's daddy was a deacon. Who was goin' to believe my black ass over God fearing people? Hell I would 'a told you, but I saw the way you looked at me and Gaddis the afternoon we came to your porch after the cops had left. It was like you was disgusted at what you saw in our faces. You were right to feel that way. And you know what Gaddis said to me after we talked to your mother on the porch and walked back to across the street? He said to me, *Mercer will get over it.* What a crazy fucking thing to say."

I had no response to what I had heard. As I listened to him I understood why he didn't come forward to tell his story back then, I felt pity for Licorice and I was ashamed that I had discarded him as a friend without understanding the situation he was in. *I wondered if I was in Licorice's shoes would I have kept quiet too.*

I re-lit the joint while I was still under sitting under the tree and took a couple of tokes on the joint then handed the rest to Licorice. Licorice sat down next to me, like we were old friends again. And I guess we were. There were no words exchanged between us. We just looked over the playground watching the *ghosts* of poor black boys running up and down the basketball courts.

Chapter 30

The shifting clouds tried to hide the brightness of the full moon at dusk, a little eerie but still beautiful. I sat on my front porch alone taking in the sky. It was a warm with a breeze that carried the scents of lilac flowers in the air. It was a Monday evening and I was pondering what Licorice had confided to me the previous day about of what happened the day Smokey drowned in the Milwaukee River. I felt certain that I Licorice had told me the truth about Smokey's death. He was more likely to speak it than Gaddis Hopgood.

I thought about going back to Rutgers early, there nothing and no friends that I wanted to hang out with in this city. Besides there was nothing do for black youths to do in Milwaukee anyway. I thought about Pumpkin, and the dances we used to go to at the YMCA. I can still smell the baby powder on her soft body when we held each other tight when we kissed. I could dance a little, and Pumpkin never complained or laughed at me when I messed up on the dance floor like other girls did. I missed her a lot. Pumpkin wasn't home for the summer because she was a student in a pre-med program at Meharry Medical College in Nashville. I always thought she'd become a lawyer with the way she used to chatter constantly when we were children. I was proud of her. Pumpkin had taken a path towards her future. I had no clue as to what I wanted to do in life after college and basketball were behind me. Maybe I'd go out to California and soak in the sunshine and watch the *beautiful people* on the beaches. Smokey would've liked that. But for now I just wanted to hear the sound of Pumpkin's voice but deep down inside I knew she would never sit with me on my porch again.

My family seemed closer to me after being away from them awhile. I loved them, but didn't know how to express my love to them, maybe someday I could. My sister Birdie was a student in a state college in northern Wisconsin near Minneapolis. She was smarter than me and had gotten an academic scholarship. Birdie told me she wanted to go to college because I went. I felt good about her words.

There one person that could say "I love you" to was my *hero* Aunt Queen. Auntie taught me how to read and think beyond the conditions I grew up in. She harped throughout my childhood about the best way to get ahead in life was to get an education. Auntie was suffering with severe case of bronchitis and had moved back into our house now that Birdie and I live there for the most part. My mother took care of her and even my father did what he could to keep Auntie comfortable. I had the saddest feeling that the next time I came home from college Aunt Queen would not be with us. I spent as much time around the house to be with the woman that taught me the most about life. I yearned to get back to Rutgers where I felt my life was more substantial, but I needed to stay in Milwaukee as long as I could to be with family.

Chapter 31

A sporty looking black car rolled to a stop in from of Gaddis Hopgood's house, it looked shiny in the moonlight. It took awhile for anyone to exit the vehicle. I thought maybe someone was lost. Finally a looking stocky black guy got out of the driver's door. He headed across the street at an angle to my front porch. I knew who it was as soon as he walked under the street light. Gaddis did look different but I recognized his round head that now had thick framed eyeglasses on his face. He was maybe an inch or two taller than the last time I saw him. He was chubby, but not as fat, like he was when we were kids. Gaddis wore a long-sleeved white shirt with a dark tie and black dress pants, like he had just come from church on a Monday evening.

"Hey Mercer, Phoebe told me you were back for the summer," Gaddis said from the side walk in front of my house.

I said nothing to Gaddis, the man that I once considered a brother when we were boys. There was no emotion of brotherhood in my heart for him as he spoke to me in front of my house. I wanted to tell Gaddis that there was nothing of importance that I wanted to hear from him. But I just let him talk just like I let Licorice talk.

"Mercer, you got nothin' to say to me after all these years we've known each other? I know you blame me and Licorice for Smokey's death, but it was just an accident. There was no way to stop what happened to him, besides it was a long time ago when were kids. You can't still be holdin' a grudge against me for something that wasn't my fault."

"Gaddis, seven years is not *long time ago*. Licorice remembers that day at Estabrook like it was yesterday. He told me the whole story about what actually led to Smokey's drowning in the Milwaukee River. I tend to believe him that Smokey didn't just slip of a rock and fall in the water. That was the story you told my mother on that day you and Licorice stood in front of my house all those *years ago*."

"When did you talk to Licorice? I…I heard he was still around the city but I haven't seen him in years, but then again I was down South for a few years."

"Well Gaddis, maybe it's good you didn't see him. Because Licorice said to me that he wanted to kill you if he saw you again. Why do think he wants to do that?"

"I have no idea why'd he want to hurt me. I'm not afraid of Licorice. Plus God will protect me from people like Licorice. You know Licorice has never been right in the head. He's liable to say anything to blame me for Smokey's death. I heard he was a junkie mostly living on the streets."

"Gaddis, you seem to know more about Licorice than you led me to believe, obviously you've been keeping track of him. Licorice and I shared a joint last Sunday at the Square and he told me that you shoved Smokey off a rock in the river, that doesn't sound like an accident to me."

"So Mercer, you smoke marijuana now and I bet you drink alcohol too. Growing up you was too afraid to do bad stuff like that to keep you from playing your precious game of basketball. You learned some bad habits being in college, I guess you ain't perfect. Anyway, you believe a strung out liar like Licorice rather than me? I said it was an accident that Smokey died and I stick to what I said," Gaddis said with an unconvincing tone. And I could see on his face that he was irritated and his body seemed to shake in agitation. It was Gaddis's tell; when he got upset about something when he was a boy, he became animated, especially if he was trying to hide a truth. I was glad that my words had gotten under his skin.

"I'm going to be a minister in my church soon. I'm thinking about asking Phoebe to marry me in a year or two now that she is saved. She is over Smokey's death and you and Pumpkin being off in college. I and the church members are the only friends Phoebe has now. Mercer, can I come on the porch to talk?"

"Nah Gaddis, I can hear you perfectly from where I'm sitting." I didn't want the sit next to the chubby *devil.*

"Okay, I was just going to tell you about what's going with me. I got me a few rental properties and a job at Sivyer Steel making good money. I know you saw me get out of my brand new Mustang. I'm saving to buy me a big house when my money is right. I bet Phoebe would love to live in that house with me."

Gaddis thought by mentioning Phoebe and him in the same sentence would upset me. His words were a ploy to get me angry and upset, but I wasn't buying it. Phoebe probably had no clue that Gaddis wanted to marry her. He was too selfish to be with anyone but himself. I just let Gaddis ramble on about his self and the things he has.

"You know what else Mercer? Who is going to believe a nigger like Licorice over me? He don't have nothing going on, he's just a bum. So, I'm not worried about anything he's said about me 'cause nobody will believe him, especially the cops. I've never had any trouble with the police, they don't mess with black folks like me. Another thing Mercer, I'm doing better than any niggah that ever came out of this raggedy neighborhood."

I burst laughing after listening to Gaddis praise himself. I'm thinking this Negro is full of shit. Gaddis most have drunk the spiked holy water from his church. He sounded delusional and devious. I think he was trying to impress me, but I wasn't impressed. He had nothing that made me jealous of him, not even Phoebe. And my gut feeling was that she was into church and not him. The shit coming out of his mouth was cracking me up. It made no sense for me to have a conversation with Gaddis on any topic that didn't include him as the subject. It would serve no purpose for me to engage him with any response. I didn't need any more information about the saddest day of my life when Smokey died. And I surely was over the boyhood crush I once had on Phoebe. I felt good, almost elated when I got up from my porch chair and turned my back to Gaddis standing on the sidewalk. I headed to the porch screen door and walked into my house without saying a word to him.